How To Give and Receive
Exceptional Customer Service.

CYRUS M GONDA
KALIM KHAN

EMBASSY BOOKS
www.embassybooks.in

First published in India 2008

Published in India by :
EMBASSY BOOK DISTRIBUTORS
120, Great Western Building,
Maharashtra Chamber of Commerce Lane,
Fort, Mumbai - 400 023.
Tel : (+91-22) 22819546/32967415
Email : info@embassybooks.in
Website: www.embassybooks.in

ISBN 10: 81-88452-98-X
ISBN 13: 978-81-88452-98-9

REVIEWS FOR *WHERE IS MY KETCHUP*

Slowing GDP growth rate signals an era where "customer retention" becomes more important than "customer acquisition".
This book with its real life vignettes and simple lessons is a forerunner to this trend.

Aditya Gupta
CEO - Maharashtra & Goa, Reliance Communications

The book presents some interesting customer service stories in a parable format. An easy read that will get you to view even the smallest customer request with new eyes.

Ambi M.G. Parameswaran
Executive Director & CEO - Mumbai, Draftfcb ׀ Ulka

I would rate this book captivating. Something everyone can relate to. In an era where the thrust is more on "Pushing a Product", this thought provoking book drives home the necessity of "Execeeding Customer Needs" as the prime aim of marketing. The incidents, punctuated by most appropriate quotes at the right intervals, provide a smooth narrative with a terrific punch. Cyrus and Kalim have done a fantastic job.

Commander Amit Sanyal
Indian Navy, Headquarters Maharashtra Naval Area

This book is a timely wake up call for corporate growth and success in the 21st century. It has an interesting storyline and looks at the concept of Customer Service from the viewpoint of both the customer as well as the service provider. I personally very much liked "The Message" which forms the last chapter of this book.

B.R. Jaju
CFO - Crompton Greaves

This fantastic book superbly encapsulates the customer oriented philosophy that any future thinking business needs to follow.
Kalim and Cyrus have been training my Sales and Marketing team on a regular basis and the positive difference their inputs have made is terrific.
Now they have put down their secrets in the form of a book which will tremendously benefit Indian Industry as a whole.

Jimmy Mistry
M.D. & Principal Architect - Della Tecnica Group

This is a fantastic "story" book, so easy to read, lively to the end and earthly due to real life experiences. Couldn't have asked for a better book with outstanding messages on management principles and customer service in particular. To top it, we can get absorbed into finishing reading it in a single Mumbai - Delhi flight.

L.V. Krishnan
CEO - TAM Media Research

Destined to be a classic on Customer Service from an Indian Perspective. As an HR and Training professional, I would highly recommend it as required reading for any person intending to make a career in Customer Service or Sales in any industry. There is lots to learn in this book for even a seasoned sales professional.

Neil Sequeira
VP-H.R. - Elbee Express

"Where is my Ketchup?", makes brilliant reading and gives an insight into customer service by exploring the area in depth using a very practical approach. Perfect analogy for 'catch up' makes the book compelling to read.

Sanjay Muthal
M.D. - Nugrid Consulting Pvt. Ltd.

This excellent book highlights in a remarkably detailed and insightful manner the way we all hate or love to be treated as customers. The book is full of wonderful true to home examples across the service sector. If you have a direct consumer interface and want to listen to your consumers - go grab a copy!

Shripad Kulkarni
COO - Allied Media

Any business hoping to thrive in this extremely competitive 21st century simply has no alternative but to put the customer first.

This superb book explains in a simple and beautiful form the formula for customer delight.

Each chapter by itself is worth the price of the whole book. A fantastic read.

Shhyam R. Singhania
Chairman - Enarr Capital

The next level of differentiation for all brands (not merely service brands), comes from managing the customer's experience - the proof of the pudding will truly be in it's eating. The cost of acquisition of a customer will be justified only if the customer can be persuaded to stay on within the brand's fold for a viable "life-time-value" extraction.

And in this age of constant customer churn, a well informed treatise on customer service comes just at the right time. Corporates must make this compulsory reading for their front-line managers to equip them better to manage the brand's customer equity.

The storytelling format of this book also ensures that overtly complex theory and unnecessary jargon does not come in the way of its readability, making the practical lessons contained therein easy to assimilate and remember.

Sourabh Mishra
Chief Strategy Officer - TBWA \ India Group

"Where is my Ketchup", is the perfect customer-service recipe for anyone in business today and is a "must-read" manuscript, especially for those in the service industry.

In today's world, the customer is king, lord and discerning selector from the myriad choices that he surveys.

For all businesses, big and small, the book is replete with pearls of wisdom on customer attraction, delight and retention. What makes it extra-special is the engrossing, sometimes saucy narrative which keeps the reader interested, and yearning for more! The narrative is strewn with day-to-day occurrences, which anyone from a corporate manager to a housewife can immediately relate to.

The icing on the cake (or ketchup on the samosa, if you like), is that the narrative is peppered with several pertinent, quotable quotations from a plethora of management gurus including the authors themselves.

With "Where is my Ketchup", Cyrus Gonda and Kalim Khan have served up the ideal fare for a world of commerce-centric like never before.

Vijay V. Raut
Managing Director & CEO - CDSL
(Central Depository Services Ltd.)

The authors have colorfully captured the emotions in customer service. The use of illustrations and real life events holds the attention of the reader. In a customer service oriented industry like life insurance, the message of this book is very appropriate. A wonderful easy to read book with depth of information and advice on great customer service.

Frederick D'Souza
Head - Health Insurance
HDFC Standard Life Insurance Company Limited

Customer Service ranks today as one of the most powerful business tools. Therefore it is most gratifying to see that the authors, Mr. Cyrus M. Gonda and Mr. Kalim Khan have brought out this book in a simple and highly readable language. I am sure it will be read by many and will meet with great success.

Simone N. Tata

Dedication

To

My parents Roshan and Minoo R. Gonda

for

being the best mum and papa in the world and

inculcating in me a love for books and reading.

Cyrus M. Gonda

My parents Khadija and Abdul Karim Khan

for

imbibing values that are the essence of my life

and my wife Deeba Khan

for her patience and being the love of my life.

Kalim Khan

Acknowledgements

To thank the Almighty is to do the obvious, and we would like to do that .... Also because this book is about doing the obvious.

Although cliché, but the fact is this book would have been a distant dream had it not been for the presence of some very special people in our lives who directly or otherwise contributed in their own special way. While we do take this opportunity to mention a few who have been truly instrumental in making this book see the light of day, the contribution of others not named, merely due to the paucity of space, is no less.

To begin with we would like to sincerely thank Dr. A.H. Rizvi for setting before us an ideal example of selfless service and his unconditional support in this venture. His genuine love for education and training is indeed an act to emulate. Next the two of us would fail in our duty if we did not acknowledge the contribution of Dr. C. G. D'Lima for being our academic mentor. Her zest for learning, imparting and re-learning is something that has made us better and keener students of management.

We would also like to thank all our post graduate management students whom the two of us have been teaching over the last decade across Mumbai. Needless to say but these teaching sessions did provide an immense learning experience to us. While each student has been special in their own way, this book is definitely due to the efforts of some very dear students, Furkan Shaikh, Abbasali A. Asamdi, Mohammed Osaid Koti, Mubeen Bawa and Azim N. Rizvi, who put in all their skill sets to ensure the completion of this project.

We would also like to put on record our appreciation and gratitude to all our corporate partners for whom we have been providing training and consultancy over the years. These assignments have indeed been a catalyst in initiating this project. Thanks are also due to all participants of our training programmes for sharing their valuable insights and giving us perspectives to ponder.

Last but definitely not the least two very special people deserve a mention for visualizing our dream. Thanks to Rafiudeen of Ensign Bookstore for being the channel and Sohin Lakhani for fructifying the ideas into reality.

Thanks once again….

Kalim Khan

Cyrus M. Gonda

Foreword

As the leader of numerous profit and non profit organizations, people constantly ask me the reasons why the organizations I lead are so successful.

Some people believe that success in business endeavors comes from great innovations, others feel it is dependent on luck, a third segment believe that it is the outcome of possessing vast resources.

All the above are true to some extent, but whenever I personally am asked this question I do not have to look around me for an answer. The secret of my success is very clearly known to me, so I just tell them the plain simple truth.

And that truth is, that what little success I have achieved as an entrepreneur, a businessman, and a politician, after attributing it to the Blessings of the Almighty, can be directly pinpointed to my instilling in all my ventures a philosophy of service orientation and customer focus at all levels from top down.

I truly believe that there is no alternative that the corporate world has in front of it today apart from whole heartedly devoting it's entire focus and attention on that vital and critical element-OUTSTANDING CUSTOMER SERVICE.

Be it any organization however small or large, in any industry, I can personally guarantee that in the near future, it's success and indeed it's very survival will relate in direct proportion to the thoughtful care, eye for minute detail, and the quality of service it provides it's customers, who are the organization's ONLY SOURCE OF REVENUE.

I sincerely believe that the customer, for his contribution in enabling the organization to grow, deserves the best service that the organization can provide.

This excellent, captivating masterpiece of a book more than lives up to it's promise of understanding the concept of customer service from both ends, the Service Provider's as well as the Customer's, and not only educates organizations and their staff how to give better and better service, also at the same time it opens the eyes of customers to the world class standards of service that a few successful organizations are providing today.

This book apart from being a joy to read for it's interesting storyline and element of humour, is an object lesson to us all that what one needs to provide memorable service is not vast resources or latest technology, but a generous heart.

I am proud of the fact that this book which clearly brings out this need of the hour and is a timely wake up call for the Indian Corporate World, has been authored by Kalim Khan, the Director, and Cyrus M. Gonda, the H.O.D.- General Management, of the Rizvi Management Institutes.

Dr. A.H. Rizvi

President	*Former Member of Parliament*	*Chairman & Managing Director*
Rizvi Education Society	**Rajya Sabha**	**Rizvi Builders**

Preface

A customer is the most important visitor on our premises. He is not dependent on us. We are dependent on him. He is not an interruption of our work, he is the purpose of it. He is not an outsider to our business, he is a part of it. We are not doing him a favour by serving him, he is doing us a favour by giving us an opportunity to do so.

— Mahatma Gandhi

Indians should be proud that the best and most apt quotation on the need and importance of focusing on the Customer has come from the pen of the Father of our Nation, Mahatma Gandhi. The words he said so many years ago are as relevant, if not more relevant, today.

The last few years have seen such a rapid increase in the awareness levels and demands of the Indian consumer, it makes one's head spin.

More and more people than ever before are experiencing Air Travel, using Resorts as Weekend Getaways, visiting Malls for their shopping needs, picking up exotic foodstuff from the local Bakery, eating out at Deluxe Restaurants and Hotels, sending their parcels and mail by Courier, using Credit Cards and other services provided by Banks, depending on Mobile service providers for communicating and staying in touch, joining Gymnasiums to work out and stay fit, and on and on and on.

The eyes of the global economy are on India, and it is in the service sector that we have the best chance of making our global mark. It is the sector where maximum openings for jobs could be created.

But this potential can only be realized to it's fullest extent if the focus is not merely on service, but on quality service that must be so outstanding that it becomes legendary and memorable, the impact of which is so positive on the customer that he automatically becomes a fan, then an advocate and ultimately the advertising voice of the service provider, cementing the relationship so solidly, that not even the rise of a thousand competitors can damage that relationship. Indeed service by itself has no meaning or value unless it comes from the heart. If it does not, neither is it appreciated, nor is it remembered fondly and definitely does not translate into growth and profitability for the service provider in the long term.

Indeed though the quantum and volume of the service sector is increasing rapidly, unfortunately the same cannot be said about the quality of service nowadays. It is a rare commodity and exists in isolated pockets and islands, and wherever it is found and experienced, the happy customer rests there and crowds it like an oasis of refreshing water among a largely unfriendly desert lacking the same attraction.

The signs are all around, and getting stronger by the day.

Courts are daily awarding increasing damages to aggrieved consumers, where they have been offloaded by airlines after holding confirmed reservations, or when their complaints about defective televisions and washing machines have not been handled promptly and courteously, or where banks have not followed the correct procedure but sent goons to residences of people who have slightly delayed repayment of their loans, or against courier companies for misplacing important documents, the list is endless and increasing exponentially. Even the media is giving more and more prominence to these issues on the front pages.

Customers also have memories more powerful than the proverbial elephant when it comes to remembering both good and bad service. In fact very recently after it was reported that a group of bus conductors ganged up and beat a schoolboy who didn't have the exact change to buy his bus ticket, a reader wrote in to a newspaper saying he could empathise with the boy as a similar incident had **occurred to him thirty years ago and it was still as fresh in his memory as if it had happened yesterday.** And it is not only physical pain which is remembered. The mental pain and trauma that accompanies rude, indifferent and lethargic service is equally if not more engrained in the memory, and future actions of whether to go back to that service provider, are very often decided on these issues.

More and more people are taking time out from their busy lives to write letters to newspapers about bad service they have received, which is an indicator of how strongly they feel about the same. Whether it is an airline making them endlessly wait while the flight is delayed, many passengers have written in to say that it is not the delay per se which is agonising but the total lack of communication and concern from the airline staff that upsets them more. Or letters from mobile users complaining about loss of data during data transfer from one phone to another because of carelessness of the staff. Or customers endlessly being made to wait on hold listening to repetitive music, and then getting cut off after being on hold for half an hour. Every industry has more than it's share of dissatisfied, disgruntled customers, who swear never to come back again, and spread the negative word to as many people as they can by all means at their disposal.

Is all this important? You bet your business and your livelihood that it is. In fact it is **the most important factor** in any business. Peter Drucker, the guru and great grandfather of modern management thought has stated in very clear terms that the single most important area of focus any business in any industry must have is **customer retention**.

Logical. Very logical. We have all heard of the statistic that it is five times cheaper in terms of time, money and energy to retain an existing customer than it is to attract a new customer. But if we look around, literally every marketing activity today is focused on attraction rather than retention.

And for every such aggrieved customer who writes a letter to the press, there are thousands more who feel the same way and are spreading the negative word about their service providers in their large circles. Like many service providers say when a customer complains, "you are the only customer who has complained," as if it's only counted as a complaint if ten other people have taken the effort to complain as well. In fact you should be thankful to the customer who has complained, as he's taken the time and effort to give you valuable feedback. Another well researched statistic also tells us that 98 % of customers who experience poor service don't complain, **they just don't come back**. Today people have many groups, both social and professional, to which they belong. Office, clubs, neighbours, relatives, friends and other acquaintances, are all social networks where people share and discuss their experiences they have had with their service providers.

In fact, a well known socialite has gone on record saying, "Whenever there is a lull in a conversation at a party, I get the talk flowing by just mentioning an incident of poor service I recently faced, and everyone rushes to add their own stories."

Globally, corporate houses, big and small, have given the highest priority to customer relationships, investing billions in the effort to train their staff to be more responsive to customer needs.

In fact in a recent global survey, A T Kearney Consultants asked CEO's of 463 of the world's leading companies to rank as to what they felt were the most critically important concerns for their business.

The results of the ranking in priority order were as follows.

1. Customer Relationships

2. Cost Competitiveness

3. Effective use of Information Technology

4. Change Management

5. Shareholder Value

6. Revenue Growth

7. Industry Restructuring

8. Globalisation

9. Value Added Relationships with Suppliers

See the ranking.

It hit us with the force of a level 5 tsunami when we first saw it.

These were the leading and sharpest corporate brains in the world, and what they have unanimously put as their number one priority is customer relationships.

All the financial parameters; Cost Competitiveness, Shareholder Value, Revenue Growth, are no doubt important but they come later in the hierarchy of priority for these CEO's. Makes sense, doesn't it? Without satisfied customers there wouldn't **BE** any shareholder value or revenue growth in the first place.

These are the CEO's of the very same global corporates who are eyeing India very strongly as a market with a huge potential. And whether it's a product or a service these companies specialize in, at the end of the day it is vital to remember that today, no job is a product job, every job is a service job, and only the percentage of service in the job differs. These global corporates will very soon be entering India, e.g. Walmart, and they would definitely focus on providing customers with a superior service experience. If by that time we as Indian service providers have not woken up to the need of the hour, we would be left standing, with no one but ourselves to blame.

This book is our contribution towards the wake up call for Indian industry which is urgently required.

Between the two of us as co-authors, we have trained over a lakh of corporate participants and management students and have learned as much from them as hopefully they have learned from us. We take this opportunity to sincerely thank each and every one of them from the bottom of our hearts. Over this period of time we have come to the conclusion that it is nothing but a customer oriented attitude and an eye for the smallest detail that guarantees success to any organisation over a period of time. The examples which we have conveyed in this book in a story form are based on actual incidents which we have either experienced ourselves or have heard of from delighted or disgusted friends, depending on whether the service they received was excellent or atrocious. The names and locations of certain individuals and organisations have been changed, but the basic incidents have their footing in ground reality, which is where the learnings hopefully come from.

Any organization, large or small, in any industry, can tremendously benefit from the deep rooted lessons and learnings in this book, and we would be very happy if we manage to, through our message, be the catalysts to spur Indian industry on to its rightful place as a truly world class benchmark for services, thus fulfilling the dream of The Father of Our Nation.

Happy Reading.

Contents

The Headache

Today's customers call the shots.
They no longer have expectations.
They have demands.
And if you don't meet their demands, they will find
another supplier that does.

- Larry Hochman

"That's the tenth complaint we've had about the caterers this month, and the month is only five days old. I'm fed up," yelled Apurva, the G.M. - Administration of Sunshine Ltd. "I can't get any of my other work done. Seems that all my time I'm just a complaint box for that bloody canteen operator. Why can't he improve his service?"

"What's wrong, boss? Seem to have a bad day?", asked Rajeev, who was more a friend than a subordinate to Apurva.

"You know we've kept a caterer so that our staff can avoid meal time hassles of carrying a tiffin box or gorging themselves on unhygienic fast food, but this caterer is more of a headache than he's worth. I can't take it any more. Either he goes or I go. We're giving him business of a thousand meals a day including breakfast, lunch and dinner and he's charging us around 50 bucks a meal and he gets 25 days of business a month. That's a bill of Rs.12,50,000 every month. The guy's getting a crore and a half of business from us every year and he is treating us like dirt. Instead of ensuring that complaints don't come in the first place, he is on the contrary lethargic and allows the same problems to occur over and over again. Even when we complain, it's like yelling in one ear and out of the other. I have got him here to keep our staff happy and well fed and not to add to our miseries."

"Then why don't you do something about it?", intervened Rajeev.

"But what can I do? Looks like I've run out of options. These damn caterers are all the same. I've tried out almost every caterer in the yellow pages over the last two years. They promise you the moon when they first start off and within a month's time the quality of food and service deteriorates so much, they behave as if they are serving free food at some charitable home."

"Chill man, you'll get a stroke. Have a coke. Top it with rum. Why are you getting worked up?", that was Rajeev again, who was the cooling influence on his boss. "Lay your problems on me, man. What's the problem these guys are laying you with? Tell me nice and easy. I want to understand your problem in detail."

"Okay, I'll tell you. If it's not one thing, it's another. I'll tell you some of the complaints about the caterer reported time and again by our staff.

Either the chapaties get over early, and half the guys don't get them ...OR...

He takes away the lunch sharp at 1.45 which he says is the time mentioned in his contract, and doesn't even wait a minute after that. Our staff who are busy with a client can't just leave the client half way and when they come to the lunch room the lunch is gone. Vanished. ...OR...

The gravy is bloody like water ...OR...

The food's so spicy we just can't have it ...OR...

The plates and glasses haven't been properly washed and are greasy and dirty ...OR...

Half the time, the food is stone cold. The guys don't take care to heat it up ...OR...

He promises a salad daily but now invariably one or two days a week the salad is missing and he gives some lousy innovative excuse. I wish he was so innovative in preparing his menus ...OR...

He initially used to provide different varieties of rice dishes, e.g. A biryani one day, a fried rice the next, tomato rice the third, jeera rice the fourth. Now it's just plain boiled white rice everyday and even that isn't cooked well ...OR...

The lunch arrives late. I don't see why when the famous Mumbai Dabbawalas can be on time everyday ...OR...

It's less chicken and more bone in a chicken dish ...OR...

The dessert portions keep getting smaller and smaller ...OR...

I am sure they add extra names, more than the people who actually had lunch, to inflate the lunch bill and then they want their bill paid promptly on the 1st of every month without giving us time to tally the number of meals consumed in the month. I wish they were so particular when it came to supplying the meals on time.

And these are just some of the complaints I am swamped with. You want me to carry on? I am already out of breath. I think I need that rum and coke right now. I get the shivers just thinking of how these guys treat us. And they're our suppliers. Yet they act as if they're doing **us** a favour."

> *Great things are not done by impulse, but by a*
> *series of small things done together.*
>
> - Vincent Van Gogh

"But how did you come to appoint these caterers in the first place?", asked Rajeev.

"These guys have apparently come with excellent credentials. I never even bothered to check them out. Guess they're forged as well. And they advertise big time in the corporate papers. I think that's where they pour in all their money and don't have anything left over to provide good food and service. They attract clients through their ads, build up expectations, and then bring the expectations crashing down."

> *Let us not live in word, neither in tongue,*
> *but in deed.*
>
> - Bible, 1 John 3:18

"But is this issue really worth boiling yourself over?", queried Rajeev.

Apurva replied, "My main concern is that a well fed employee is a happy employee. He gives out his best. It's like if you had attended a wedding yesterday, and if the food was good, you would tell your friends that the whole wedding was great."

"On a festival day, our office staff eagerly wait to see what's provided by the caterer on the table. If the lunch is not upto the mark, down goes the enthusiasm and the morale we strive so hard to build. Then the bitching and the backbiting starts. "The management doesn't care"; if only they knew how hard I'm trying and breaking my head with these caterers. Even on a normal day, the staff spends at least half an hour cribbing about the lack of taste or not getting to taste a good dish because it was in short quantity. After paying these caterers the price they demand, you'd think that they'd at least provide half of what they promise."

"I've noticed that the graph of food and service quality drops drastically within a month after a new caterer takes over. There's absolutely no consistency in their delivery. They just want to impress us for the first fifteen days, and then they start to show their true colours."

"As I said, I have on an average a thousand staff daily from Monday to Saturday having their breakfast, lunch or dinner in office. Lately it's got so bad that staff who never before had carried their lunch are now starting to carry their tiffins or going out to grab a quick bite like a sandwich. And people are starting to pass sarcastic comments that as a G.M. – Admin, I'm not even able to locate a single good caterer in this great big city. The message is going around that the caterers are able to get away with all this because they're giving me a kickback. It's affecting my reputation. The staff doesn't realize how I've been breaking my head with these caterers to get them to run the lunchroom smoothly without any complaint."

"I feel like quitting my job. It's getting that bad. Instead of the caterers trying to please our organization, after all it's WE who're paying the bill, and it's not a small bill either, here WE have to spend our time running after THEM. Having heard all this, now do you have any suggestions?"

"Sure," replied Rajeev. "Don't I always have suggestions? There's this terrific restaurant called 'The Great Taste' near my house that's opened around six months back and they serve a really tasty meal. I've heard that they've recently opened a Corporate Catering Division. I'm sure their service ought to be great. Always wanted to suggest them to you, but I didn't want to interfere as I have always carried my tiffin for health reasons. Anyway, you need to relax. Why don't you come with me today evening and we'll go to 'The Great Taste' for dinner? You need a break as well and it'll be a good opportunity for you to check out their food and service. Wrap up your work, give me a call and we'll go there and solve your problem."

The Meal

"Okay, Rajeev, I'm done for the day," said Apurva later that evening, sounding exhausted. "Let's get moving and check out this miracle restaurant of yours. I'm really looking forward to a good meal. I'm glad it's a Sunday tomorrow. We can have a nice leisurely dinner and relax this evening. Hope the guy in charge there turns out to be half as good as you say he is. It'll solve a long standing problem for me."

"You know something, Rajeev," continued Apurva. "I've always believed that it's the philosophy and attitude of the man at the top of the ladder that percolates down to the bottom most level. I hope the owner's around today. If he's there, maybe we could speak to him and get the ball rolling."

"Righto, I think he should be there," said Rajeev. "It's a long time since we've gone out for dinner together. We'll take my car. I'll ring right now and book a good table."

At seven they left the office. The traffic was worse than usual. They reached the place by eight. There was a smart valet in a sparkling uniform who gave them a crisp salute and took their car away to park.

"Nice décor," said Apurva, glancing around the restaurant as they entered. "Impressive. I'm building up an appetite already."

Their table was ready for them.

"Hey, nice menu card, really innovative. It's made of wood and hand painted," noted Apurva.

The manager of the restaurant came to their table, acknowledged Rajeev, and was introduced to Apurva. He asked them their preferences and offered suggestions. They sat back admiring the ambience. Good paintings on the walls. Very nice polished teakwood furniture. The owner appeared to have spent a lot in doing up the place. The restaurant was starting to get filled up with people starting to walk in. There was nice soft music playing in the background, just the type of music that Apurva enjoyed. He started tapping his feet and humming along with the music; he looked totally relaxed. The cutlery and plates laid out were very classy.

The food arrived and Apurva took the first bite. Yum.

His taste buds sang. The air-condition was just at the right temperature. The sofa was really comfortable. He was just hoping that he could meet the owner before the evening was over. He was ready to finalise the deal on the spot at an even higher rate than he had paid any of the previous caterers. The guy managing the place sure appeared to know his job.

The meal was over. The manager suggested a dessert which he claimed was the speciality of the house. People came from far and wide to sample it. "It's a brand by itself, please try it."

"Sure," said Apurva. "Whatever you suggest and your chef can whip up is bound to be great."

It was. It was pure heaven. Melted in the mouth. It was playing havoc with his diet but what the hell, you only live once, and meals like this didn't come on a daily basis.

"Another dessert?", smiled the manager knowingly.

"Sure, let's indulge. Bring it on." It arrived promptly and went down the stomach smooth as silk.

They paid the bill. Apurva was purring like a contented cat. His only regret was that he couldn't take up permanent residence in this place.

"I'm sure this guy's corporate meals will be a pure delight if this meal experience is anything to go by," Apurva told Rajeev.

They rose from the table and were about to leave the place when the owner, Mr. Chavan, walked in. He greeted Rajeev, who was obviously a regular there.

"You're just the person to make the evening complete," said Rajeev. "I'd like to introduce you to Mr. Apurva, who is head of administration in our organisation. I'd spoken to you about him and the requirement that may turn up for our office catering."

"Oh yes, I remember," said Chavan. "We're really focusing on the new Corporate Catering Division. It's the new baby in our family and I want to see it grow. If you have some time, why don't you step into my office and we can chat?"

"Sure," said Rajeev, turning to Apurva. "That's just what we were looking forward to ourselves. We've got all the time in the world. Tomorrow's a Sunday. So we're in no hurry. I've promised my boss that I'll solve his problem and I've never let him down so far. I feel I'm the official trouble shooter in the organisation. Let's wind up the issue tonight if possible. We can always work out the details and draw up the contract later, right Apurva?" They walked into Mr. Chavan's plush office. They sank into luxurious soft chairs.

"Scotch?", asked Chavan. Rajeev nodded on Apurva's behalf as well as his own. Apurva was suddenly looking a bit low, but Rajeev put it down to work stress and the recent heavy meal.

"Scotch?", repeated Chavan, glancing at Apurva, "or could I offer you something else?"

"Uh, no… Scotch would be fine, but just a very small one," said Apurva, hesitantly.

"Sure you're feeling okay?", Rajeev asked him.

"Yeah, yeah, I'm fine. It's just been a hard week at work. I'm fine."

They chatted for a few minutes and then Apurva got up to leave.

"Great guy, wasn't he?", Rajeev asked Apurva as they both left Chavan's cabin and sat in the car. "Great food too. I told you I'd solve your problem." He paused for Apurva's answer. Apurva was silent and had a glazed look in his eyes.

"Hey, what's wrong with you? You sure you're okay?", asked Rajeev.

Flashback

Apurva wasn't listening to Rajeev. His mind was floating back fifteen years into the past, back to his management college days.

Yup. It had been a good time. Years of bliss with good friends. Not the kind of stress the way he was experiencing now. Sure, there were exams and stuff, but compared with the type of pressures he was going through currently, that was chicken feed.

As he floated back in time, his thoughts focused on his college canteen. Stale sandwiches and sickly sweet tea. That was about the full extent of choices available there.

So everyday he and his group had to decide where they had to go for their snacks or their lunch.

They tried Ali's biryani joint one day, Sam's fast food the next and Chong Lee's Chinese Shack on a third.

A dreamy smile came over Apurva's face. All the good memories came flooding back. Yes, his group had definitely enjoyed their college days.

Then his face clouded over. Another dim distant memory surfaced.

And it wasn't a pleasant one.

Ali, Sam and Chong Lee's smiling faces slowly faded away, and another face, an unpleasant one, a face that smiled with the lips but not with the eyes, seemed to emerge.

He tried to recall what was familiar about that face. A face that seemed to hold such unpleasant memories for him. His head started to ache.

That's when Mr. Chavan had courteously asked him if he was feeling well? Would he like him to call the doctor?

"No, no, I'm fine, guess it's just the work and lack of sleep. I'm sorry, but could we put this discussion off to a later date? I'm not in a state to discuss anything right now," he heard himself apologise.

"Of course," said Chavan smoothly. "I quite understand. Business always has to be discussed with a cool head. Please rest and then we can meet up and finalise the contract. I would love to be of service to your organisation. Could I offer you the use of my car to drop you home?"

"No, it's quite alright. I'm feeling much better. But yeah, some rest would do me good. Thanks for the hospitality. It was an excellent meal."

Somehow, he didn't quite know why, he just couldn't bring himself to say that he'd enjoyed meeting Mr. Chavan. He just couldn't get himself to speak those words. He didn't know what was wrong with him. How could he forget his manners like that?

Apurva left Chavan's cabin with Rajeev and after the air conditioned confines of the restaurant, the fresh cool air of the night brushed his face like a soothing balm. He started feeling better immediately.

Then it hit him.

That face from the past with the unpleasant associations it brought.

It merged with Chavan's smooth smiling face.

The voice from the past blended with Chavan's oily voice.

Then the incident from the past started to unfold in his mind.

It had been a college day in his past like any other.

He along with Sunil, Priya and Radhika had all got fed up of Fast Food and Chinese Food and decided to try the new restaurant that had recently opened near their college.

It looked pretty good, but seemed to be an expensive restaurant, and with their limited pocket money during college days, if they had their lunch there, it meant the next two days would be sandwiches and tea in the college canteen. But what the heck, life's meant for living, right?

They had bunked the last lecture of the day and walked over to the restaurant. An attractive sign board announced that it served Indian and Chinese dishes. Were they hungry? You bet. They walked in and looked around and selected a good table. The waiter handed them the menu and they studied it more avidly than they studied their text books, taking their time. Lots of Chinese and Moghlai dishes as well as Continental and Fast Food dishes were represented in the menu. They glanced at another waiter carrying over a plate of biryani to a guy on the table next to theirs. Man, it smelt good. They no longer felt the need to look at the menu. They'd made up their mind.

Biryani for all of them. Sunil and Priya ordered chicken biryani, and Radhika and Apurva himself being vegetarians ordered a veg biryani each. The price was higher than they'd assumed, so instead of the next two days in the canteen, they would have to spend the whole week there. But at least they'd enjoy themselves today. That was the important thing. They'd been planning on coming here all week and now they were finally here.

They placed their order and then started to observe the décor.

The place was well done up. Nice tasteful music playing, not too loud and not too soft. The waiter's uniforms looked smart. Very nice place mats and glasses.

Their order arrived. The steaming hot biryanis were placed in front of them and the smell of the burnt onion rings which garnished the biryanis wafted deliciously to their nostrils and made them all salivate.

Then Radhika, who knew Apurva and his tastes as well as she knew her own, (today she is his wife), gestured to the waiter and asked for a bottle of tomato ketchup, without which no meal was complete for Apurva. Minus ketchup, even the best cooked dish simply did not go down his throat. For him, it added that final zing, the missing link, like the secret ingredient in Coca Cola. It enhanced the taste of all food that he ate. It was a habit and taste that he had developed in childhood, when his mother literally had to force him to finish his meal. One day in desperation she had added some ketchup to the rice and gravy he was playing with, and like a miracle cure, he was hooked. He gulped it down. From then, no meal was complete for him without the divine ketchup.

Fish live in water. Men die in it. Nature is diverse, and not all tastes are the same.
— Zhuang Zi

Radhika requested for some ketchup and was amazed at the response from the waiter.

"Sorry madam, we don't serve tomato ketchup with biryani."

The waiter's tone was polite, but his message was very clear.

Radhika was upset and adamant, but the waiter was as obstinate as a mule. She asked exasperatedly, "Surely such a big restaurant stocks some tomato ketchup?"

"Oh, yes, definitely, madam, but it's served with pizzas, burgers, sandwiches and such dishes. We do not serve ketchup with biryani. **It's our policy."**

Voices were raised, guests seated at other tables started to focus their attention to the ruckus going on at their table.

A man in a suit, apparently the owner or the manager, briskly walked over and asked the waiter at their table what the chaos was all about.

"Sir, they ordered biryani, I served it, and now they want tomato ketchup with it," said the waiter in a tone which indicated that he thought they were partially insane. "I explained to them that we don't serve ketchup with biryani, and that's the reason they're upset. You yourself had told us during our training which dishes we should provide ketchup with and which dishes we shouldn't. That's what the problem is."

"If that's all that the problem is about, then let me tell you that the waiter is absolutely right," said the owner or manager, whoever he was. **"Whoever heard of having ketchup with biryani?"**

> *Do not do unto others as you would have them do unto you. Their tastes may not be the same.*
> - George Bernard Shaw

"**We did**," said Radhika, really upset by now. "Are you going to dictate to us what dishes we should have ketchup with? Are you deciding our taste for us?"

> *Don't try to tell the customer what he wants.*
> - Gene Buckley (Sikorsky Aircraft)

"You can drink plain ketchup for breakfast, lunch and dinner at home for all I care," said the owner/manager rudely. "You can satisfy all your weird tastes somewhere else. Normal people don't have ketchup with their biryani. No customer has ever made such a request before. When I price the menu, I do it on the basis of food cost. The costing for biryani does not include the cost of ketchup. If you want an explanation why we are refusing to serve you ketchup with your biryani, that's it. Try running a business yourself and then you'll understand what I'm saying."

"The menu does not mention that ketchup is to be provided as an accompaniment for biryani. Now please continue with your meal. You're disturbing the other guests. If you so badly want ketchup I can provide you some in a bowl, but I'd like you to know that you'd be charged an additional Rs.5 for that in your bill. Ketchup has a cost, you know?"

This may seem simple, but you need to give customers what they want and not what you think they want, and if you do this, people will keep coming back.

\- John Ilhan

"I can't believe this man," said Radhika. "Come, let's go back to college right now and have a sandwich in the canteen. This man has totally ruined our meal and our day. I don't want to even breathe the same air he's breathing for a minute more."

"You can do as you please," said the owner, "You can finish your meal or leave it uneaten, it's all the same to me. But whatever you decide to do, there's the matter of a bill to be paid for what you've been served. You ordered it."

"I can't believe this man's human," said Radhika, shaking her head in disbelief. "How can he talk and behave that way with his customers?"

She opened her purse, removed a 100 rupee note (each biryani cost Rs.25. This was 15 years ago), and said, "There's your bloody money for your bloody bill."

"Madam, I request you to mind your language," said the owner.

"Yeah, sure, a guy like you talking of good language. You don't deserve to run a restaurant. In fact you shouldn't be in the service industry at all. You're inhuman," said Radhika, almost in tears.

As all four of them stormed out, with all eyes on them, they heard the owner softly laugh, no doubt pleased that he'd made them pay for a meal they didn't eat.

They all went back to the college canteen and had sandwiches and tea. All day long they just couldn't seem to speak of anything but the sick attitude of the owner of that restaurant.

Apurva wished he could have struck him. The guy had the nerve to insult and humiliate Radhika in public. And they were supposedly guests. That's what the food industry called its customers, right?

> *"Would you refuse a guest at your house some ketchup with his biryani if he wanted it?"*
>
> - Cyrus M. Gonda & Kalim Khan

Now it all came back to him. The face of the owner of 'The Great Taste' was the same face he had just seen, only 15 years older.

It was Mr. Chavan.

The same owner they'd just met.

No wonder it brought back such unpleasant memories. This man had been responsible for one of the most humiliating experiences of his life. And his wife's as well.

And over such a trivial issue. How much worth of ketchup would he have consumed with his biryani anyway?

He shook his head as if to clear away the unpleasant memory and came back to the present.

Rajeev looked concerned. "You're sure you're okay, dude? I mean your face looks white. You're sure you don't want to see a doctor?"

"No, just drop me home. I just feel I need some rest. Had a hard week. I'll be fine tomorrow."

They were both silent on the drive all the way home. There was no traffic on the road at that hour and they reached Apurva's place in fifteen minutes.

"Good night," said Rajeev cheerfully. "See you on Monday and let's wind up the contract with this guy as soon as possible. I can't wait to have meals like this every afternoon. I'll even stop carrying my tiffin."

"Yeah, sure, we'll see. Good night. Enjoy your day off," said Apurva as he entered his house.

Radhika was waiting up for him and seeing his face, knew there was something on his mind.

"What's up, all fine?", she asked.

He nodded. "Just something which isn't worth bothering about right now. I'll tell you all about it tomorrow. Just need to get some sleep."

She knew that he needed to rest and though she was curious to know what it was all about, she decided she could wait till the next day.

4
Next Morning

Next morning Apurva woke up late since it was a Sunday, and sat down to have a leisurely breakfast, the one day in the week he had this luxury. He had his newspaper in front of him and was casually scanning the cartoon section.

Radhika was brimming with curiosity and as soon as he was through with the paper, she reminded him that he was going to tell her something interesting today.

He nodded, recollecting the events of the previous evening and the memories they had evoked.

He started by relating the problems he was having in office in trying to locate a good caterer.

Radhika was already aware of that since it was an ongoing problem, and Apurva regularly shared his day's events at work with her.

Then he came to the dinner last evening and how after the great meal he had with Rajeev, he thought his problem was finally solved.

He hesitantly asked her, "You remember once in college we went out with Sunil and Priya to try that new restaurant and all of us ordered biryanis and then we had the problem over the ketchup? Do you recall that? I think we've spoken about it a few times already."

"Recall? Remember? Of course I do." Radhika's eyes were blazing. "Do you think I could ever forget that incident? That horrible man. It was one of the most humiliating moments of my life."

The guy made me feel so cheap.

"Arguing over a little ketchup and trying to dictate terms to us. And we were the customers and he was the service provider. That mean man. Of course I remember him although I wish I could forget."

> **People don't forget negative incidents, howsoever many years pass by. You as a service provider may forget such incidents and dismiss them as trivial, but your customers won't. It's affected them, not you.**
>
> - Cyrus M. Gonda & Kalim Khan

"Anyway, what about him? Why did you bring him up? You were talking of the great food you had yesterday. What's that got to do with him?"

"Yeah, it's sort of connected. Rajeev took me to a restaurant for dinner since I was looking out for a good caterer. This restaurant he took me to has started a Corporate Catering Division and we went there to check out the food so I could get an idea as to how their corporate catering would turn out if we decided to select them as our office caterers."

"So?"

"So the food and service were great but------- ."

"But what?"

"But when we were leaving the restaurant, the owner walked in, and he knew Rajeev, so Rajeev introduced me to him and we went to his cabin to sort of talk over the catering contract for our office. I didn't know why at that time, but something just didn't feel right."

"Rajeev was urging me to take a decision on the spot and work out the details later and to be honest I was tempted to do just that. I wanted to get the whole thing over with as well. But something held me back. Something which I couldn't put a finger on just then. **Kind of a blast from the past.**"

"I left the cabin and came out into the fresh air trying to recollect where I'd seen the owner's face before and------ ."

"And don't tell me, let me guess, it was that same creep?" Radhika had always been a smart girl. She was good at putting two and two together.

"Yup, right you are. It was him all right. I didn't tell Rajeev about it because he was really keen on getting this wrapped up. So I just told him I was too tired to decide just then, and he drove me home. So that's it."

"Oh," said Radhika. "No wonder you were looking spaced out last night. Yuck. Even the thought of that man puts me off. How could someone be so cheap? Anyway, let's not take too long over breakfast. I've got to get the house cleaned up. Hope you haven't forgotten that we've invited our MBA college gang over for dinner tonight. You chill, enjoy your Sunday. I'll get things organized. There's not much left to be done anyway. If you could just step out and get some nuts and those tangy wafers that Harsh likes so much, I'll take care of everything else. They're going to be here around seven thirty."

5

The Get Together

The Sharmas, Mistrys, Shaikhs and Nayyars arrived one by one.

"Hi, good all of you came. Been such a long time since you've all been here," welcomed Radhika.

She loved having people around her and she was a very friendly and emotional person by nature.

Rashi sat down on her favourite chair.

"I just love this chair. Such a unique piece of furniture. And so comfortable. I'd love to have one like this at my place."

"Thanks," said Radhika. "It's been in my family for generations."

"I know all your favourite drinks and have them all ready. But if you want something else, just let me know," said Radhika, always the perfect hostess. "There's vodka for Harsh, orange juice for the saintly Furqan, red wine for Priya, and of course scotch for Sunil."

The glasses were on the table. The nuts and chips were brought out.

"Cheers," said Apurva, "Here's to the long and strong friendship we all share."

Gradually talk got around to work issues and the stress and problems all of them were facing at their work place. Radhika prompted Apurva to tell the others his problem with the caterer and of course the unpleasant reunion with that beast, Chavan.

"Eh, Sunil. Do you recall the fight that we had for ketchup after bunking that boring Economics lecture by Manjrekar?", started Apurva.

"Of course," said Sunil. "That's where we saw the angry young Radhika in action for the first time."

"You know it's not something one could forget, right?", added Priya holding Radhika's hand.

Apurva then carried on about how difficult it had been to locate a decent caterer who could sustain his quality over a period of time.

"Its plain sickening that each of the caterers turns out to be worse than the other. And at first glance they all project themselves to be so good. They look so promising when I initially meet them and have a food tasting session with them. The dishes they make me try are always so tasty."

"Yeah," said Rashi. "That's always the problem. The taste is one part of the meal, but the main ingredient is love."

If the vital ingredient of love is missing, the relationship will not last.
                    - Cyrus M. Gonda & Kalim Khan

"Perfect," said Rahul. "Your love gets reflected in my growing tummy size."

"Wish Ushma knew how to cook what others could eat," remarked Harsh.

"We'll discuss that when we get back home," got back Ushma.

"Now don't start that fight again. Why don't you learn from me and Farah the art of being a perfectly married couple. There's only one secret, I dictate and she obeys," intervened Furqan.

"Why don't you guys come and meet Furqan at the hospital tomorrow," fumed Farah.

"Good nurses, I don't mind…Eh, but Apurva you were saying something when these stupid girls intervened. Go ahead man," said Furqan.

"Nahi yaar. It's not the bad quality of food by different caterers time and again that bothers me so much. It is their disgusting attitude that irritates me more."

Excellence is not a skill, it is an attitude.

- Ralph Marston

"Damn it. How can a person be a part of the service industry and carry an absolutely lethargic attitude to serve.? **I thought a healthy attitude by itself was the most important ingredient in the dish called service," spoke Apurva with a lot of passion.**

"Boss, you should go back and take lectures in our college," joked Sunil.

"No no, jokes apart. I think what he is saying makes a lot of sense," intervened Rahul. "Aren't we all at the receiving end of shoddy services from service providers in almost all our interactions as customers? And guess what, that too, in this era of cut throat competition. Amazing."

"But what surprises me more is no one seems to be bothered about this inspite of the fact that there is no rocket science attached to it," added Rashi.

"Come again? I didn't get that," remarked Farah while helping herself to some chips.

"What I mean is we all know that in this day and age, there is no substitute to customer service. And that it is only service which enhances the relationship between the seller and the buyer. Isn't this the only thing taught in almost all management classes? And yet do we see this in practice? I can at the drop of a hat narrate multitudes of instances where the service provider has even verged on the extent of being downright rude, callous and demeaning," opined Rashi.

"The only face that comes to my mind over and over again is that creep of a Restaurant Manager," fumed Radhika.

"But he is not the only creep," added Harsh. "What Rashi says is right. It takes efforts to provide immaculate service… But what I have inevitably experienced over and over again is plain lethargy and a book full of excuses in the garb of policy to avoid even the bare minima in the name of service."

> *Freely have ye received, freely give.*
>   - Matthew 10:18

"What's wrong man, you've really got serious," asked Sunil, as he sipped his scotch.

"Okay, let me narrate this incident and see if you can control your temper," added Harsh.

"Fine. But hold on, before you start let me get some starters," said Apurva. "And of course a lot of ketchup."

"You know what, something just struck me. I am sorry Harsh, but before you begin I have to share this with you. You guys know how I forget things," intervened Rahul.

"Go ahead," said Harsh.

"What I feel is good service in any industry is like ketchup served. The ketchup by itself does nothing, but it's absence is definitely felt. What we've experienced frequently as customers is always the missing ketchup," said Rahul, beaming with pride at his own insights.

> *Statistics suggest that when customers complain, business owners and mangers should get excited about it, the complaining customers represent a huge opportunity for your business.*
>   - Zig Ziglar

Think of giving not as a duty but as a privilege.
- John D. Rockefeller Jr.

Giving presents is a talent; to know what a person wants, to know when and how to give it, to give it lovingly and well.
- Pamela Glenconner

You make a living by what you get. You make a life by what you give.
- Winston Churchill

6

The Resort Agony

"We can recall this incident which stands out in both our minds like a sore thumb," said Harsh. "You know what I'm talking about, right sweetheart?"

"You mean Alibaug? (Alibaug is a suburb of Mumbai). Sure I do," said Ushma. "That's **OUR** ketchup and I've lost count of the number of times and to the number of people I have mentioned this. I never get tired of talking about it. I really would like the world to know this so that the damn resort runs out of business. I'm sure I've told you guys about it, but maybe not in detail."

> *Treat every customer as if they sign your paycheck, because they do.*
>
> - Anon

"Here it goes," started Harsh.

"It happened a couple of years ago at New Year. We were wondering where to go to get away from the city and finally planned to spend the New Year at a resort for a change. We scanned the newspapers for all the New Year offers and packages and finally decided upon a package at a resort on the beach at Alibaug. It was a Rs. 19,000 package for a couple for the 31st and the 1st with all meals included. The photograph of the resort in the paper looked terrific. Just what we needed. The resort faced the beach and the rooms shown in the ad also looked tastefully done up.

We both love the seaside so we rang up and booked a deluxe room. Since the full amount had to be paid in advance, we paid by credit card. We drove down and reached the resort on the evening of the 31st just as the sun was setting."

"Breathtaking. We were going to love this place or so we told ourselves. Our batteries started to get recharged almost instantaneously," added Ushma.

"The room we were allotted was nice and cozy. There was a plasma TV in the room just as the advertisement had mentioned. Not that we were planning on watching television but the guys had really spent on doing up the place," continued Harsh. "We both took a leisurely shower together after a long time. Hey, why are you blushing?"

"You are crazy," laughed Ushma.

"So what? We're among old friends. And it was the 31st after all. Anyway, after the shower we went on to the balcony of our apartment and gazed up at the stars. After sometime we went back into the room, decided to have a scotch from the minibar in the room before going down to the buffet room for dinner. We had a drink each and opened a can of chips to go with it.

Sipped, munched and chatted. We had really needed this break. Pure heaven.

Before deciding to go down for dinner (it was around 10:30 p.m.), I wanted to call Dad. We always feel guilty about leaving him alone although he is very sweet about it and says it's our age to enjoy life.

I used my cell to call him, couldn't get through, and suddenly realized why I hadn't received any calls in the last five hours. I wasn't getting network. Being alone with Ushma after such a long time had completely taken my mind off my mobile phone. I asked Ushma to check her cell for network and she was not getting network either.

Well, can't expect everything away from civilization. Anyway, we could always use the hotel landline. I dialled zero for the operator as the hotel directory next to the phone indicated and requested for a call to Mumbai.

The operator was polite and sounded sweet and I told her that I needed to call Mumbai and asked her the dialing procedure. **She said Dial 022 followed by your Mumbai number and you will get through.**

I got through immediately and spoke to dad. I asked him if he had finished his dinner. Ushma then spoke to him as well and wished him a Happy New Year in advance. We both spoke for just about a minute because dad said you guys spend time with each other. You can always chat with me tomorrow. That's dad. Sweet as sugar.

We hung up the phone and decided to call Ushma's aunt as well. She is also an old lady who stays alone and her kids are abroad. We got through to her without disturbing the operator this time as we just dialed 022 and then the Mumbai number, just as the operator had instructed.

I think the poor aunt was already asleep when we called her but she was delighted to receive our call. Again we spoke for less than a minute and then hung up. Now no more calls we told ourselves, as we gazed at each other.

In a way it was a blessing that our mobile phones were out of coverage area. No one could disturb us with New Year greetings now. I had already given dad the number of the resort we were staying at in case of any emergency before we left home, so that was fine.

It really was a beautiful resort, with around a hundred bungalows and apartments daintily laid around the seafront.

We debated whether to call for some food in the room and not go down to the dining hall at all, but then decided against it primarily as both **Ushma and myself like our food and especially chapatis piping hot, otherwise we don't enjoy our meal.** And whenever we had ordered food from room service in the past it invariably was cold by the time it reached the room.

So although we wanted to spend as much time alone with each other as possible up in our room, we decided to go down, have a quick, hot dinner and come up to be by ourselves. **We weren't really too concerned what the menu was as long as it was served hot.**

That's what we wanted.

Do you know what your customers really want?
What you consider as not that important may be the
VITAL INGREDIENT for them.
We all are unique individuals and have our own
different tastes. That's why every menu has so many
alternatives.
We're not all machines, made in the same way,
running on one common battery, or petrol or
electricity.
Pick up nuances from body language, words, tone
and gestures and customise your offerings.
The word CUSTOMISE – comes from the word
Customer.

- Cyrus M. Gonda & Kalim Khan

We quickly put on some casual clothes and walked down the flight of stairs to the banquet room where the dinner was already in progress. Seems like the other guests had the same idea of grabbing a quick meal downstairs and then going back to their bungalow or apartment before midnight.

There were around 30 people already seated at tables when we walked up to the buffet.

It smelt good. We were glad we had come down to the dining hall. **Food always tastes so much nicer when it's hot.** And apart from lunch the next day this was the only meal we were going to have here and we had paid Rs. 19,000 for a day's stay.

We wanted to enjoy this meal and were already anticipating going up to our room in about 20 minutes. We wanted to skip rice and the dessert. **Just a couple of piping hot chapatis and some vegetables**

was all we wanted. We took our plates and walked up to the buffet counter. There was no one ahead of us in the buffet line and I glanced at the chapatis in the dish. There were around four or five hard and dry looking chapatis left. I gave them the benefit of the doubt and picked up one to see if it was actually as hard and cold as it looked. It was cold and stiff. There was a hotel guy standing nearby. (Later we came to know that he was the owner's cousin).

I smiled at him. He stared back at me vacantly. I requested him to come over where I was standing. Somewhat reluctantly he shuffled over. He glanced at me as if upset that I had disturbed him. I told him, pointing out to the buffet dish that held the poor chapatis. **"Sorry to bother you, but if there's one thing I like with my meal, it's having my chapatis nice and hot.** These look like the end of the pile. I don't mind waiting a couple of minutes if you would kindly arrange a few hot chapatis for us. Four should be just fine. It would be so kind of you if you could do that. I'm not a rice eater and chapatis are my favorite. Good hot ones, those too."

God knows I was polite.

Can you guess the reply?

"If we start making and serving fresh hot chapatis to everyone in the line, who is going to eat these? You expect me to throw these away?"

And he turned and walked off leaving us speechless. It was obvious to us that as far as he was concerned we could have cold chapatis, or none at all.

There was no third option.

> *Regardless of the size of a service company, a high degree of customer satisfaction will be maintained as long as employees at all levels remain mindful of the maxim that "the customer is always right". If you determine that a customer is not right, then for all intents and purposes you have already terminated your relationship with that customer.*
>
> *- John Olsen, Chairman & CEO,*
> *Cunard Cruise Line*

And to top it all there was no one in the line behind us. No one else could have heard us and started getting ideas and demanding fresh chapatis like we did, if that was what worried him.

Well, as far as we were concerned that was the end of New Year's Eve for us. It was nearing 11 p.m. We quietly ate a few vegetables without any chapatis to accompany them. Although the Gulab Jamuns served for dessert were my favorite sweet, we were so upset off we just couldn't eat a bite.

I must say through all this that the rest of the staff looked very polite and sympathetic but couldn't do a thing as the owner's cousin superseded them all.

Like in the story of Alladin, the genie of the lamp supersedes the genie of the ring.

> *An Attitude of service orientation in any organisation has to flow from top down. It can never be bottom up.*
>
> *- Cyrus M. Gonda & Kalim Khan*

We went up to our room and I slammed the door and lay flat on the bed with my shoes still on my feet.

Ushma asked me to remove my shoes as they were spoiling the bedsheets.

I yelled at her. Asked her to shut up as I wanted to make that bloody bedsheet as filthy as I possibly could.

> ***Never underestimate the power of an upset customer.***
>
> > - Anon

And as far as I recall I got really nasty with Ushma.

That is my memory of our New Year's Eve.

Ushma started crying and I went out on the balcony looking out at the dark sea, my thoughts as dark as the sky and the sea themselves.

Ushma quietly read a newspaper in the room and after some time the light in the room went off. Presumably, she tried to sleep.

I stayed outside still thinking. Is this what we had come here for? Spending 19,000 rupees to fight with each other, and for what? **It wasn't her fault, and I'd yelled at her just because the guy in the buffet room who was supposed to make our stay a pleasurable one had messed it up with his rude and inhospitable behavior.**

How the hell could I have allowed a cold chapati to ruin our well planned New Year's Eve like this?

But then, **I'm only human**.

And this type of nasty attitude from a guy whose job it was to look after my comfort would have tested the patience even of a saint.

But that wasn't all this resort had to offer.

The icing on the ketchup bottle was due the next morning at checkout time.

I must have slept at around 1:30 after watching fireworks going up all around, hearing the ship horns blow at midnight as they traditionally do on New Year's Eve, and everybody (except the two of us), bringing in the New Year.

I cursed the day that I'd ever seen the advertisement of this damned resort and lay awake tossing and turning all night. I must have at last got some sleep towards dawn. When I woke up it was 9:45.

Ushma was looking at me as I opened my eyes. I immediately sprang up, hugged her, apologized and wished her a Happy New Year. She hugged me twice as hard. (Don't know where she found the strength, she'd hardly eaten anything the previous night).

She asked me to forget everything. Have our breakfast and leave the damn place as soon as possible. Can you believe it? She had already packed for departure.

I decided to take a quick shower and the only thought that kept coming to my mind was a wish to have no problems with the breakfast.

They had already screwed up my New Year's Eve. I wouldn't let them ruin the first day of my New Year as well. Even if they gave cold soggy toast, I would accept it, is what I had decided.

We entered the dining room for breakfast arm in arm, giggling like a couple of teenagers.

The room was empty. Then it struck us. Of course, we were the only ones who had slept so early. The others would be so fagged out after having danced all night, the only meal they would think of next would be a leisurely late lunch.

So we could have the breakfast hall to ourselves. Great.

I ordered a cheese omelette and Ushma had scrambled eggs. There was ample toast (hot), and I had porridge and Ushma had honey cornflakes. We washed that down with a nice tall cold glass of orange juice each. That felt goooood.

We could barely get up, (we were so stuffed), and once again walked out arm in arm to settle our bill.

There was no one in the line at the cashier's counter either. We could just pay our dues and move out of there. At least the day seemed to be going well. The only thing we would have to pay for would be the items we had consumed from the minibar the previous evening and the two local telephone calls we had made which I had almost forgotten but Ushma reminded me about.

Well, the calls shouldn't be more than 10 bucks, we didn't even speak for a minute each and they were local calls, I told her. Let's see how much we owe for the scotch, the soft drinks, the snacks and let's move.

"Apartment number 22, could we have our final bill please?", I requested the person at the cashier's counter.

"Certainly Sir." He punched some keys and the bill started to print. "Here you are Sir, hope you enjoyed your stay." He handed me the bill in a leather folder.

I glanced at it.

What ?????

"Hundred bucks for two local phone calls which did not even last a minute each? Have you guys gone crazy?", I shrieked.

The cashier glanced at the bill I thrust back at him and calmly replied, "Those weren't local calls you made Sir, they were national calls."

"But I just dialled Mumbai which is a local call from Alibaug. It's just that I wasn't getting a signal on my mobile so I used your hotel phone."

"Here, Sir," he held out a tariff card.

It read :

TELEPHONE TARIFF

Local calls	Rs. 7 per minute.
National calls	Rs. 50 per minute.
(Inclusive of service charges and taxes)	

"But I'm telling you I only made two local calls not exceeding a minute each. I owe you Rs.14 and not a paisa more.

You've already screwed up my New Year's Eve. I'm damned if you screw up my New Year as well. Here." I removed Rs.14 in exact change and banged it on the counter.

"I'm sorry Sir, I can't accept this nor can I release your bag from the Luggage Counter till you clear your bill as per our records."

I was ready to explode but Ushma held my hand and went forward.

"Can you please explain to us how your record shows that we made two national calls when we know that the two numbers we dialled were local Mumbai numbers. Alibaug to Mumbai is a local call."

"Sure, Ma'am, here are the two numbers you dialled. You dialled both the numbers to Mumbai, which would normally be local calls, but you dialled them starting with a 022. The moment you dial any number starting with a Zero, it becomes a national call and you are charged accordingly. I agree the numbers are local Mumbai numbers but you should not have dialled 022 before dialing them. You should have dialed 9522 and then the number. Then it would have been registered as a local call. Both methods would have connected to the same number."

"But when we asked your operator how to dial a Mumbai number from the room telephone, she was the one who told us to dial 022 and then the number. She should have guided us properly," fumed Ushma.

"I am sorry Ma'am, that operator has finished her shift and gone on a fortnight's leave starting from today. Anyway the fact remains that you owe us the amount of Rs. 100 for the service you used. As a cashier, that is all I can tell you."

"Do what you like. Just try and stop me," I said and I went to the baggage desk, picked up my bag, literally dragged Ushma with me, went to the car, started it, and went down the driveway.

We reached the exit gate of the resort and the gate was shut. There were two security guards at the gate. There was the cashier, running down to the gate towards us along with a fat guy in red bermudas and a parrot green T-shirt. They reached us huffing and puffing.

"What's the idea behind all this?", I demanded. "Why are the gates locked? What's the problem?"

"I'm the owner of this resort," parrot green T-shirt said pompously. He looked irritated as if he had just been woken up. "You owe us Rs. 100 and you tried to run away without paying it. We don't allow that sort of thing over here. It's a matter of principle. I've never let anyone leave who hasn't paid his bill in full and I'm not going to start doing that on the first of January. Pay up."

Since Ushma was by now pretty scared, I tried to calmly reason with him, explaining the entire situation, hoping he would understand what I was saying. As far as I was concerned what I was saying was crystal clear, but with these guys you never know. After I explained I waited for his reaction. It was the expected one.

"I don't know anything about all that. You dialled 022 and that makes it a national call. Pay for the service you used. Till then the gates remain shut. If you can spend Rs. 19,000, why are you haggling over Rs. 100?"

"That's precisely my point," I said. "I am not haggling. If I could pay Rs. 19,000 for a night's stay, and I've paid that in advance, why would I crib about Rs. 100? I'm a guy who leaves a tip of Rs. 100 for a Rs. 500 meal if the service has been good," I said.

> *Customer complaints are the school books from which we learn.*
>
>   - Anon

"I don't know about all that," he repeated. He was yelling by now and his red face matched his red bermudas. "You pay me the money. I'll make sure you're blacklisted and you won't be allowed to set foot in any of my resorts ever again."

In spite of my anger, I burst out laughing.

"You mean to say you own some other resorts as well? Please let me know which ones they are so that I and all my friends can blacklist you," I said in return.

I didn't want to carry on with the situation further because Ushma was panicking with all the WWF type security goons glaring at us. I threw him a 100 rupee note which one of his goons picked up and handed to him. After suspiciously staring at it to make sure it wasn't a fake note, he ordered the gates open.

Well, that's it. The 2 hour drive back to Mumbai was like an escape from hell.

I repeat this incident to whoever I can and I've kept the detailed bill with the phone charges as a reminder of the worst New Year I ever had.

> *Some organisations don't fix the problem. They fix the customer, so badly, that the customer never comes back.*
> — Cyrus M. Gonda & Kalim Khan

I wouldn't recommend anyone to come to this resort, even as a last resort.

I could have shot the guy at that moment if I had a gun," said Harsh, revealing the depth of his feelings.

"That is very unlike you Harsh. Remember Prof. Gupta would always call you the kind hearted guy," teased Rashi.

"If that be the case then you must have realised what a demon that parrot green T-shirt must have been," retorted Harsh.

> *Customers may forget what you said, but they will never forget how you made them feel.*
> — Anon

"Okay, let me change the mood a little bit. I think we've all got a little too negative. I still think there are some organisations who provide fantastic service and that indeed is their USP. In fact it is mainly their service which gets customers coming back to them," said Priya.

"Whom are you talking about? Does such a species exist?", smiled Rahul sarcastically.

"Fine. Then what I narrate now is a fantastic positive ketchup and it has also got to do with hot chapatis," smiled Priya.

"Have you heard of this restaurant called Govinda?", she asked.

"Ya ya. It's the one inside the Iskcon Complex," jumped Rahul. "What amazing food man."

"Yes indeed the food is great... In fact it's delicious... But that's not what I want to tell you. Just listen to this terrific incident. The other day I went there for dinner and as you mentioned about your resort, there were just a few cold chapatis left in the serving dish here as well. I asked the supervisor if I could have some hot chapatis please."

He politely folded his hands in a gesture of namaste, said, "I'm so sorry you had to tell me. I should have noticed and restocked the dish myself. Pray give me a couple of minutes. No need for you to wait at the counter, I'll have them sent to your table." He rushed to the kitchen and within a couple of minutes got me 3 hot chapatis on a side plate at my table, apologised once again, and said, "Anything else you need just let US know."

> *Note, the word is US and not ME. Excellent service should always be first system and team dependent, and then person dependent.*
> — Cyrus M. Gonda & Kalim Khan

After the meal I met him and thanked him for his hospitality.

He said, "Not at all. **Our concept is very clear. Food is Krishna Prasadam. To be relished and praised and enjoyed.** Not wasted.

If it is cold and not to your liking, you may eat half and waste the rest and it would not be your fault, because food cannot be had cold. **And we would be committing a sin."**

> *Our greatest asset is the customer, treat each one as if they are the only one.*
> — Laurice Leitao

"Even I had a terrific experience at Govinda," said Apurva. "I was waiting there with a friend to collect a parcel order and in the meanwhile asked for a glass of water. Although juice was not part of the parcel menu, juice was offered to both of us, even though only one parcel was ordered and my friend Sohel was just accompanying me. The waiter said, **"Please try our special varieties of fruit juice instead of water."** They didn't charge for the juices although 2 full glasses of juice cost much more than a little ketchup, which that creep Chavan was so miserly about.

Also the packing of the parcel was really neat and carefully done.

And instead of 8 chapatis which normally come with the parcel, they had packed 9, (yes people do count and note these things). **The staff at Govinda also listen to instructions carefully.** For example if you tell them not to pack tomatoes with the green salad, you don't have to say it twice, unlike some other restaurants, where even if you specifically order a vegetarian dish, you sometimes end up being served chicken. It's so irritating when people don't listen to instructions carefully."

> *When people talk, listen completely. Most people never listen.*
>
> — Ernest Hemingway

"Wow," was the unanimous chorus in the room, with Apurva's voice being the loudest.

"**That's healthy attitude**. No wonder they're able to get guests coming back there again and again," continued Priya.

"**Two similar incidents about hot chapattis and handled so differently.** The resort which charged Rs. 19,000 for a day's stay had a horrible attitude but a restaurant which charged only Rs. 250 for a fantastic meal came off with flying colors," added Sunil.

"No wonder Govinda Restaurant is always packed with happy smiling customers, and recently they have shifted to a larger premises in the same complex to accomodate the ever increasing guests," said Apurva.

> *The most accurate Report Card or Barometer of the perfomance of a business is the intensity of the smile on the face of it's customers.*
>
> — Cyrus M. Gonda & Kalim Khan

7

The Baked Services

"Yum… These kebabs are really amazing," said Sunil gulping two shamelessly.

"What are you thinking, sweetheart?", asked Farah as she saw Furqan lost in his thoughts.

"Nahi yaar, I was just thinking about that bakery incident, contemplating whether to share it but didn't want our get- together to get converted into a negative thought sharing exercise," replied Furqan.

"In fact I think you should go ahead, because I am enjoying the discussion. What say, guys?", that was Sunil picking up another kebab.

"Perhaps unintentionally but **I think this discussion is making sense to me professionally**. I think we should all share our experiences, or rather as Rahul termed them, **Our Ketchups**. We should share these incidents not necessarily to criticize but also to learn. Let us not forget that even we are service providers to someone at our work place. The least we could do is not commit some of these service errors ourselves, lest our customers also think the same about us," remarked Apurva.

"Okay, then what are you waiting for Furqan," cheered up Priya. "Go ahead, let's hear what you have to say."

"Well," said Furqan, "Here we go... There's this pastry and sweetmeat shop that really makes TERRIFIC macaroons and bread and Bengali sweets. Their large macaroons are the speciality of the shop. People come from far and wide to pick up the stuff. But because the stuff there is so good, the rush is tremendous and the owner has not really put any process in place for serving the customers in a systematic way. My mom used to go there and since she's quite old and short, even though she used to reach the counter first, the college crowd that used to barge in later literally used to push her aside and shove their long hands over the counter, yell at the top of their voice, grab the attention of the guys behind the counter and get their orders served.

Elderly people were just not only **not** given priority, even though they were first in line, they were just plain ignored. This is the first negative ketchup in this experience made up of ketchups that this shop seems to specialise in.

One day there was a small party to be held at our place and one of the guests who had been invited had simply loved the macaroons we had served the last time he had come over. As my mom is very particular, she kept reminding me to ensure that I got four packets of those macaroons on the day of the function. Each packet contained four macaroons and cost Rs.20.

I had a vague idea that the macaroons did not come in to the shop too early. Since the shop is pretty far from our place, I went there around 11 a.m. so as not to disappoint mom. I had to reschedule my work at office to do so, but luckily my boss is pretty understanding as he knows my mother quite well.

I went there at 11 a.m. and the shop was comparatively empty for a change.

I breathed a sigh of relief, hoping I could get it over with soon. Because of the mad rush and the disorganized system, I hated going to that shop almost as much as I dreaded going to the dentist.

I handed the guy behind the counter a 100 rupee note and asked for four packets of macaroons.

"Not come as yet," he mumbled, **without glancing up.**

"Uh oh. When are they expected?", I asked politely.

"Don't know," he mumbled again.

All this time the manager of the shop was watching from the cash counter, not saying a word.

"I'm sorry, but I need four packets for a function and I have come all the way just for the macaroons. Can't you at least tell me what time they will come?"

"Normally around 1:30," he said, as if it pained him to open his mouth.

"So if I come at 1:30 I would get them?"

"Not sure," was his bullet point reply.

"What do you mean?", I again asked patiently, taking care not to irritate him as he already looked to be in a bad mood.

"Sometimes 1:30, 2, sometimes 2:30, you try," he said, again without looking up.

"Can I get them by about 4:30 if I come to pick them up? Do they remain till that time?", I asked.

"Don't know. Sometimes all sold in five minutes."

"Okay. Do me a favour, keep this 80 bucks, I'll come around 4:30 and pick up four packets," I told him. I thought I'd come after work and pick them up.

"Sorry, can't do that," was the second ketchup splashed on my face.

"You don't have them now and it's already 11 am. You can't tell me what time they'll come. You can't tell me what time they'll get over. You won't take the 100% advance I'm giving you and reserve them for me. **Do you expect me to hang around your shop all day to buy 4 packets of macaroons?** Why can't you keep this money I'm giving you as an advance and reserve them for me? What's the problem?", I yelled, seemingly on ears that were voice proof.

"You think we can remember in all the rush to keep aside your macaroons when they arrive? If I forget to keep them aside, you'll yell at me. That's why I am not taking an advance," got back Mr. Defence.

"But why should you forget?"

"I'm human."

"Can't you note it down and keep it?"

No reply from Mr. Defence.

"I want to speak to the Manager," was the only remedy that came to my mind while I was trying to control my temper.

"The manager is there. You can speak to him if you want to."

The manager, although obviously listening to all that was going on, since the shop was still empty (guess the regular customers knew that the stuff arrived when the day was almost over), was acting as if he was absorbed in reading a book, which unless he was a magician, I don't see how he could have read, as the book was upside down. It was obvious that his attention was on us, but he pretended that he had not heard our exchange.

I told him exactly what I told the guy on the counter, ending by requesting him to take my money as an advance and to reserve the macaroons for me.

His answer was definitely not encouraging.

"You can come like everyone else and TRY YOUR LUCK. **Don't teach me how to run my shop.** My products are the best. I use the best ingredients," was the bottle of ketchup hurled at me.

"Yes," I said, "That's exactly the point. It's because your product is so good that I'm requesting you. **Why do you mess up such a good product with such lousy service?**" And I walked out.

But I knew that I couldn't go home without the macaroons since I had promised my mother. I rang my boss and explained the situation. He sympathized. "Why don't you hang around there, have your lunch, pick up the macaroons when they arrive and take the day off? You needed a break anyway. You've been working too hard."

"Thanks a ton, buddy, that's why I love working with you," I said.

I now had a look around the nearby locality to see where to have my lunch. Nothing around was really to my taste **but since the bakery shop had literally dictated that I have my lunch nearby,** I had no options. I also kept wondering whether this cake shop earned some commission from nearby restaurants, by making it's customers wait so long that they were forced to have their meals in this locality.

I sat down at a nearby joint and had a reluctant meal.

The waiter serving me was pretty slow and I was so worried that the macaroons would be over before I reached the bakery again, that I gulped down my food and left half of it on the plate and rushed to the shop at 1:25.

> *Make your product easier to buy than your competitors, or you will find your customers buying from them, not you.*
>   - Mark Cuban

"Not arrived still," said the guy at the counter, "Try after half an hour."

"Okay Boss, I'm at your mercy."

I went out in the blazing sun again. I remember it was the merry month of May. I did some casual window shopping in a nearby mall with my mind still stuck on the macaroons and came back to the shop by 2.

The macaroons apparently had arrived as soon as I had left and were almost over.

I managed to get four packets, considered myself fortunate, and handed over a 100 rupee note.

"It's 80 for four packets," I was told.

"I know that," I said. "I've given you a 100 rupee note."

"Give change," said the guy at the counter, handing me my 100 rupee note back.

Grumbling, I removed Rs 80 in change and gave it to him.

He handed me the four packets in my outstretched hands and I clutched them as if they were solid gold.

"Can I get a plastic carry bag please," I requested, wanting to get out of the crowded store as soon as possible.

Apparently everyone had been waiting for the macaroons to arrive and had all barged in together.

"Plastic bag given only for purchases over Rs.100. Your bill was only to Rs. 80."

"WHAT?" I couldn't believe my ears. I was a regular customer. I had always run up a bill worth more than Rs. 100. On this visit here, I had waited for three hours to pick up four packets of macaroons,

I had to take the day off from work, I had been treated rudely, and now I couldn't even be given a carry bag?

"I'll pay you for it," I said. " Just gimme a carry bag. How do you expect me to carry this?"

"You should get a bag with you when you know you're going to make purchases. **Our policy is fixed. We don't sell bags. We sell macaroons.** Please move, you're blocking the counter."

> *As a service provider, you will not even remember to whom you were rude, but the recipient of your rudeness will remember it for a lifetime.*
> - Cyrus M. Gonda & Kalim Khan

Shaking my head in disbelief, clutching the precious packets and cursing slowly under my breath I left the shop. As I was leaving the shop, my mobile rang, and as I awkwardly went to pick it up, two of the macaroon packets from my hand fell on to the floor and before I could pick them up, someone in the crowd stamped on them, smashing them to pulp.

I could have wept in frustration but there was no sense in displaying any sort of emotion with these unfeeling, uncaring people, who selfishly centered all their systems around their own convenience.

I went back to the counter clutching my two remaining packets even tighter. I wouldn't mind dropping my mobile phone but I couldn't risk dropping the packets of macaroons.

"Two more packets please," I said handing him over Rs. 40 in exact change.

"Sorry, macaroons are over. Just sold out."

They had remained in the shop for precisely 15 minutes.

Heartbreaking. But there was nothing I could do. I walked out in a daze, still nervous about dropping the remaining two packets. Luckily outside I met a street vendor from whom I also used to buy stuff regularly and requested him for a plastic carry bag. Although I didn't buy anything from him that day, he willingly handed me a carry bag. Luckily he wasn't bound by such RULES. I went home with the two remaining packets like a war trophy and handed them over to mom.

"Two packets? I had told you four. Can't you even remember a simple thing like that? I should have known better than to rely on you." My best answer was silence.

"Well," said Rashi, **sounds like a customer's version of Friday - The Thirteenth.** "I take it you never went back to that shop ever again?"

> *I won't complain, I just won't come back.*
> - Brown & Williamson (Tobacco Ad)

"And knowing your mom I am sure she must have given you a piece of her mind for at least a couple of weeks more," said Rashi.

> *More business is lost every year through neglect than any other reason.*
> - Jim Cathart

"Wild horses couldn't drag me back to that bakery again," said Furqan. "But I do pass by there once in a while and I noticed about six months after this incident occurred with me that another similar shop opened up right next to it. Out of curiosity, I went to try it out.

The products in this new shop were just as good but the ATTITUDE and SERVICE were STREETS ahead. Pleasant smile, taking orders with an advance, giving you a receipt for it, phoning the production department and finding out exactly how long a product would take to arrive if it wasn't already there and giving you accurate information, not asking you for change like a bus conductor, giving plastic bags whether you buy one packet or ten, and you know what? Gradually that old store which used to do roaring business, behaving like a lame tiger without competition in the jungle, is now starting to wear a deserted look."

"Hey, I have got a similar story," said Rahul.

"Who can stop you from speaking? Go ahead," said Rashi.

"There is this very famous bakery in Nashik. This bakery is really famous for its biscuits and cakes. People actually made it a point to plan their trip to this shop while in Nashik. Further this shop was on the top of the list when it came to shopping for festivities and special occasions. Their products were really excellent.

But since the past few years many people who went there told me that the famous biscuits and cakes get over as early as 7:30 in the morning. Even if they reached there around 8 a.m., all their products were sold out.

"Come tomorrow morning by 7," the disappointed customers are told.

In effect, their most famous products are only available for around an hour and a half each day, that too at inconvenient hours.

Even if the owners feel they're satisfied with the profits they make and don't need more (assuming they're God's good men), that's not the point.

> *You can't disappoint your loyal customers who are making an extra effort and going out of their way to patronise you. It's like showing a candy to a baby, making it salivate and drool and then sadistically pulling it out of reach.*
> - Cyrus M. Gonda & Kalim Khan

All the positive word of mouth publicity and loyalty that has been generated as a result of creating a superior product is flowing down the proverbial drain.

Anyway, if what you make gets daily sold by 7:30 a.m., obviously if you make a little more it will not go waste. Make a little more one day, then a little more the next, and soon you arrive at a good judgement. It should not take you more than a month at the most if you are genuinely interested in your loyal customer's welfare. But this problem has been going on for years with no one bothered.

Another negative ketchup is that this shop has a large long counter with a big frontage where about 10 customers can stand at the same time. There are only about two guys on an average behind the counter even at peak hours to service the customers. They don't bother about who has reached the counter and ordered first. If it is a frail old lady with a weak voice near the counter, even if she has reached there first, she's going to be ignored till kingdom come.

Here it's a case of might makes right.

The Law of the Jungle is obviously what the owners believe in.

A tall, hefty customer with a booming voice and arms like a gorilla can come from behind, pick up his order and move away, maybe even reach home, consume and digest the cakes, have his nap, and the old lady in front may still be left standing, waiting for her bread and biscuits.

Because of this callous, unfeeling and primarily arrogant attitude, in recent years many imitations of their famous products are being made by other people whose approach towards customers is far better.

Clear case of customer going out of his way to show loyalty but getting in return the reward of a *Kita* (kick in the ass).

After all how long can a smitten suitor keep adoring his beloved if she continues to behave badly. Even if she is the most beautiful woman on earth, the man looks for someone maybe less beautiful but with a better heart and a kind and understanding nature.

"Hey," said Apurva. "Let me add on about my experience at Famous sweets again at Nashik. It is a very well known sweetmeat shop and perhaps attracts footfalls equivalent to that of pilgrimage centres in and around Nashik.

I had gone to Nashik for an official visit and five people from my office had requested me to get sweetmeats from that shop for them.

I went there, picked up the stuff, and had to wait in a long queue for payment.

It was monsoon time and it had started drizzling outside the shop.

I wanted to get this shopping over with as soon as possible as I had come on a business trip and was on a tight schedule.

I picked up 5 packets of 1 kg each for the 5 people and a 1 kg packet for myself. After all I had heard so much about the great quality that though I am not very fond of sweets I couldn't resist trying them out. They were pretty expensive but everybody had raved about their quality being terrific.

I waited in the long queue and mentally calculated the total amount (6 kgs @ Rs 550 a kg), and kept seven notes of rupees 500 ready.

Even as the longest night has its dawn, my turn at the counter came at last.

I handed over the packets and the money to the cashier.

I also gave a bright smile to the cashier (partly out of relief for having got through the line). Either my smile went unobserved or the cashier felt it wasn't worth returning. Maybe I should get my teeth cleaned.

Man who can't smile shouldn't open shop.
                                             - Chinese Proverb

"Six separate bags please for the six boxes," I said, making what I thought was quite a reasonable request.

I had to tell him this as I noticed him cramming all six packets into one bag as if aiming for a Guinness record for maximum boxes fitting into one bag.

He stared at me as though I were demented for asking for such a favour.

"They're to be taken as gifts for six different families," I explained hurriedly and guiltily.

The way he glared at me as though I were a criminal with a fascination for plastic bags, and that I'd spent all my time in the queue merely to cheat him out of his treasure, I felt I had to justify my supposedly eccentric behaviour.

"Not my problem," he barked. "If it fits in one bag, I'll put it in one bag. **How you give it to other people is your problem. One bill, one bag, that's our policy."**

> *Courteous treatment will make the customer a walking advertisement.*
>
> - J. C. Penney

"Oh," I said. "One bill, one bag. So every time I make a purchase and pay you, you put it in a separate plastic bag, right? So, if I buy one packet at a time, stand in line 6 times, then I'll get each packet in a separate bag, right? That's how your policy works?"

His sadistic reply was, **"If you have the time to stand in line 6 times, go ahead."**

"Isn't that ridiculous and a lose-lose situation?", I asked. "I waste my time, you'll waste your time by making 6 separate bills and having 6 transactions instead of one, attending to me 6 times, your other customers will also have to wait longer while I take my extra turns, and at the end of it, you'll still end up giving me 6 separate bags anyway. All I'm requesting you is to give them to me now itself and everyone saves time and effort."

"Listen, you can do what you like. **I don't care if you get delayed or the other customers get delayed. I have to finish an 8 hour shift and whether you alone come 100 times or 100 customers come one time each, my job remains the same.** Preparing bills. I have my instructions given very clearly by my management. Now do you want one packet now and want to come back five more times for the rest or do you want all six packets in one bag now? It's all the same to me. Decide fast, you're holding up the others."

Well, I know that you can't win an argument with a human donkey, especially a donkey whose master is an even bigger fool than he is, and I had other business to attend.

I didn't have the luxury of an eight hour shift to attend to the same customer a hundred times like he had.

What idiotic management allowed a front line man to hold such ideas in his head and proudly flaunt them at customers, I wondered.

I walked out into the drizzle, and I still had one more task in this city to complete. I had to pick up a few packets of butter biscuits, again for friends who had requested me, which a small bakery nearby was well known for. Hoping it wouldn't be another nerve shattering experience, I reached there after asking for directions. The drizzle was still light.

I looked at the bakery. It was an open frontage on the street. Nothing much to look at. Nothing glamorous about the signboard on top. No neon lights. In fact the paint on the old signboard was peeling. But there were lots of people standing near the frontage waiting to make their purchase.

I moved closer.

A simple glass display with normal looking bread, cakes and biscuits in simple packaging. It was clean and neat to look at but definitely not eye-catching or extremely attractive.

I wondered what was so terrific about this small place that a couple of people from Mumbai had specifically requested me to even go a bit out of the way but definitely pick up cakes and biscuits for them from here, as well as try them myself.

Then I observed the people behind the counter. Both were slightly elderly gentleman in simple shirts. Both were slightly unshaven and had stubble on their chin but I doubt that was done to keep in fashion.

Then I noticed something else.

The customers waiting to be served were all smiles and some of them were laughing out loud.

I wondered what the joke was.

I looked back again at the gentlemen behind the counter and observed them more closely.

Grey hair, kind twinkling eyes, one had an impishly grinning mischievous face and the other had a rather lost, comically sad expression.

For some reason they reminded me of Laurel and Hardy.

Then I paid attention to what they were saying.

I noticed that there was a connection between their speaking and the happy faces and smiles of the customers patiently waiting in front of the counter.

The old guys were joking, passing humorous remarks, (not insulting anyone in the process), and everyone was thoroughly enjoying the exchange.

I noticed that even customers who had been served and had paid their bill still hung around and waited back to listen to the good humored talk of the old gentlemen and see the comical expressions on their faces. It was like having a free ringside seat at an A-grade circus.

> *Do what you do so well that your customers will want to see it again and bring their friends.*
> - Walt Disney

Then I noticed something more.

The old guys, while appearing to be very casual and unconcerned, were actually very sharp.

They kept track of exactly who came to the counter first, and although the customers were spread all across the counter, they served the people who had had come first, first. And unlike the previous place where the elderly customers were pushed around by younger guys and ignored by the so called "service staff" behind the counter, here the elderly were given preferential and priority treatment and served first, even if they had walked in later.

> *Be everywhere, do everything, and never fail to astonish the customer.*
>
> - Macy's Motto

The old guys behind the counter jokingly told the other customers, "Let us serve these senior citizens first, please wait, we'll serve you a cup of tea and a fresh bun for being so patient." Or to a youngster, "This is how we treat our senior customers, if you keep coming to our shop, in around 50 years, you'll be eligible for this special treatment as well."

And nobody minded.

In spite of the rush, the old gentlemen handled things calmly and efficiently, and at the same time put everyone at ease.

It was like a large happy family and the two guys behind the counter were the jovial Santa-Clauses, the father figures.

> *Customers are like a swarm of bees, without the honey there is no attraction.*
>
> - Ifeoma Mbuk

"In the other shops you guys spoke about," continued Apurva, "You could see the stress the customers went through to make their purchase and then move on. In those other shops, it was a chore.

Here, the purchase was an enjoyable experience that regulars looked forward to. And no split air conditioners, softly piped music, etc. were necessary to create this ambience."

> *These guys were their own portable ambience, creating an electrifying atmosphere through their kindness, customer focus, empathy, efficiency and humour.* *THERE IS NO AMBIENCE BETTER THAN THE HUMAN TOUCH.*
>
>   - Cyrus M. Gonda & Kalim Khan

I stood there entranced.

Words cannot do justice to that experience.

It had to be participated in to be believed.

Later on, after speaking to some of the customers who appeared to be regulars, I found out that this was a daily ritual played out three to four times a day when the fresh bread and cakes were baked.

People knew that the bread got baked and **was ready at a certain time each day, like clockwork**.

Unlike the uncertain, unsure, try at 1.30, 2.30, who knows, God knows, type of behaviour experienced elsewhere.

These simple guys realised the value of their customers' time.

Here, the bread got baked and was ready **exactly** at 7 a.m., 10 a.m., 1 p.m. and 4 p.m., **on the dot, each day**. A Swiss Watch could be put to shame by their punctuality.

And, surprisingly, the regular customers, inspite of knowing this, made it a point to come to the bakery half an hour before time, to chat and share in the jokes and humour.

For many regular customers, it appeared that buying bread at this bakery was the highlight of their day. Better than any reality comedy show on television.

"Yes please, gentleman, what can I do to be of service to you?", Laurel asked, bringing me out of my daze at witnessing this experience, so simple yet so uplifting, **almost like a spiritual experience.**

Like getting a high without drugs.

> *Great Service is addictive for a customer. He will stick like glue wherever he gets it.*
>
> - Cyrus M. Gonda & Kalim Khan

I broke out of my thoughts and said, "I've come from Mumbai. A couple of friends requested me since I was coming to this city to get some butter biscuits and your famous tea cakes for them. And I would like two packets of each for myself as well please."

"Certainly, gentleman," said Laurel. "Is this the first time you are visiting our bakery? I don't recollect seeing you here before."

Sharp observation and keen eye are a necessary essential in any service industry.
- Cyrus M. Gonda & Kalim Khan

At the other bakery even though I'd gone there 20 times the guy behind the counter wouldn't recognise me from Adam, **as he never bothered to look the customer in the eye and greet him anyway.**

"Yes," I said. "This is my first visit here."

"And if I can manage it, I'll come here as often as possible," I immediately thought to myself.

"Aah. Then you must allow me to gift you a small packet of our most famous cheese biscuits to take home with you. I know you'll love them," he said. "Just think of it," he continued, "My cheese biscuits travelling all the way to Mumbai. Thank you for taking them."

"Thank you so much," was all I could say, overwhelmed with his generous behaviour.

I also noticed that he put each product that I had bought for myself and friends back home into a separate bag, without me telling him to do so.

They're for different people, aren't they?", he said. "Well, then they go in different bags. **How else could you gift them?"**

The more you anticipate your customers needs, the more indispensible you become to them.
- Cyrus M. Gonda & Kalim Khan

Then he glanced out of his shop, up at the sky, which had turned a bit more grey, **and then did the most amazing thing.**

He took back the packets he had handed over to me, put each bag into an extra plastic bag, carefully tied the top and handed them back.

Looking at my expression, he explained, "These are **MY** cakes and biscuits. They are going from **MY** bakery. They are going all the way to Mumbai. People who have eaten my products before and have obviously liked them have **specially requested** you to go out of your way to get them. **I am honoured.** You have come out of your way here when you could have gone to any other bakery convenient to you and bought similar stuff. You are personally trying my products for the first time because of the word of mouth publicity. I feel proud. Please thank the people who told you to come here on my behalf. It looks like it could rain heavily. I don't want my cakes and biscuits getting even slightly soggy. So I have put each packet in a double plastic bag and tied it on top. Now rain won't damage my products. Please enjoy them. Good day, young man. Have a safe journey and hope to see you again soon. I want to know how you enjoyed the biscuits and cakes and whether you felt the trip was worth it."

> *It is not how much you do, but how much love*
> *you put in the doing.*
>   - Anon

And saying this, he gave me a kind smile with his mouth **and** with his eyes.

A real, genuine smile, just like his products.

I walked off, literally in a daze. As far as I was concerned, even without taking a bite of a biscuit, my trip was already worth it.

> **The customer experience is the next competitive battleground.**
> - Jerry Gregoire, CIO, Dell Computers

My mental ledger started ticking.

Two absolutely opposite experiences within an hour from different organisations in the same industry.

All I could think was, the first was the devil undisguised, and the second was an incarnation of God.

Someone who not only spoke of the traditional Indian concept *'Guest is God'*, but practiced it wholeheartedly in body, mind, soul and spirit.

Compare the old gentleman's behaviour with the guy in the bakery back home.

The guy in Mumbai couldn't even care less when his macaroons were stamped to pulp in front of his own eyes in his own shop. And all this because he wanted to save on the cost of a plastic bag.

And this old gentleman, not only gave a separate bag for each packet, but ensured a second bag to keep his products in top condition.

Pride in his products, brand name and reputation.

It's obvious that for this man, his responsibility didn't end at the cash counter. It continued till the product was consumed and well digested. Unlike a chocolate brand which recently blamed it's own retailers for not storing the chocolates properly.

A mother couldn't have cared more for her child.

"Now I understand the magic of this bakery," said Apurva.

> *Excellent service means that you have done your best and utmost to ensure that your product is in top condition till it reaches the end consumer.*
>
> — Cyrus M. Gonda & Kalim Khan

Now I understood why people back home told me to go specifically out of my way to a small, unglamorous bakery **where the only brand ambassadors were the owners themselves.** They didn't need a Cricketer or a Bollywood star to dance for their product for money. They would have scorned the idea.

> *When you give away the right to an outsider who has little knowledge of your firm or it's products or services to speak on your behalf merely because the person is a celebrity in a totally unrelated field, all it shows is the disconnect between the firm, it's products and services, and the end users. The unique ingredient which no external paid brand ambassador can provide is passion and love.*
>
> — Cyrus M. Gonda & Kalim Khan

The love that the craftsman and artisan has for his creation.

Wanting it to take pride of place in any display.

These gentlemen enjoyed what they did.

They enjoyed interacting with their customers.

They entertained them without any fancy technology or plasma screens.

They took pride in their products.

They deeply respected the fact that their customers came out of their way for them.

They felt deeply honoured that their customers spread the good word about them to others.

They were justifiably proud of the fact that their customers came back to their bakery when there were so many options available.

They may have used the same quality of eggs, sugar and flour that their competitors used. Those things could hardly differ.

Their ovens may be old and not hi-tech and computerised.

Their glass counters may not be designer made.

But all these count for nothing against the vital ingredient they put in their products, that too in tons, - Love.

> *Everyone does some work or the other. There are so few who do it in the best way they can. Those are the ones who achieve success.*
> — Sadhu Vaswani

> *In the same way that you can buy a house but never a home, buy a bed but not sleep, the same way you can buy expensive technology and décor but the experience that people have cannot be bought by money. It happens because the experience people have is based on the warmth and eye and concern for detail your staff show.*
>
> - Anon

You may use the best ingredients and raw materials, imported from the four corners of the earth and the most up-to-date, modern, state of the art technology, but when that vital ingredient of love is missing, an ingredient which only you and not an outsider or brand ambassador can put in, it all counts for nothing in the eyes of the customer.

I will never forget these two gentlemen and that half hour I was privileged to spend with them.

I can still recall that pleasant scene, the happy crowd, the gentle falling rain and Laurel and Hardy.

I personally thanked my friends back home in Mumbai who had told me to get the biscuits from that shop. I will never forget that amazingly exceptional experience.

Long after the biscuits were eaten, the memory of two great human beings remains.

And isn't that what service sector management is all about?

I have become their fan. Anyone who I know who is going to

Nashik, I tell them to visit the bakery, get me a pack of biscuits and buy some for themselves, and pay my compliments to the two gentlemen.

I have visited their shop twice again and each time I have looked forward to the experience and never been disappointed. They have never let me down.

> *Once you achieve a certain level and standard of service, your customers will never tolerate or allow you to go down to a lower level again. It is your duty as a quality service provider to ensure that such a thing does not happen.*
>
> — Cyrus M. Gonda & Kalim Khan

There have been some people who have also told me to go back to that sweet shop where I had the problem with the plastic bags. My reply to them cannot be repeated in polite company.

> *A customer is really satisfied when he or she not only comes back but brings someone with them.*
>
> — Hyrum W. Smith, Chairman & CEO,
> Franklin Quest Co.

"Hey, that's superb," said Rashi. "Could you give me the address of that bakery? I'm visiting Nashik next week and I'd love to go there."

"Get some biscuits for all of us," chipped in Farah.

"It's nice to know that the basic law of nature still holds true. That there is always good to counter the bad. I actually thought there couldn't be anything outstanding about service in a bakery," added Rahul.

"Well, if you're looking for more positive balance," said Harsh, "Let me tell you about the other bakery I always patronize even though it is located out-of-the-way as far as I am concerned. It's called **Paris Bakery,** again average size, nothing glamorous, **but what service.** Whether it's the owner, or his son or their employee behind the counter, it doesn't make a difference which of them is there on a particular day. All three give the same terrific service.

Sometimes we dread going to a particular shop if a particular person is at the counter. Near my place there is a small ice cream parlour and if the father is there behind the counter, no one who knows him enters the shop. Surly, rude, bad tempered, bangs the ice cream down on the counter, won't take trouble to look for a flavour we want if it's not stored at the top of the freezer. He will mumble under his breath and sometimes loudly wondering why you can't be REASONABLE and take vanilla like everyone else which he has stocked at the top for his convenience.

His son is a cool chap; smiling, pleasant, helpful and talkative.

Again, same product, same shop, but what a difference.

Anyway, talking about Paris Bakery, they have an amazing range and variety of products, excellent quality, all the stuff available throughout their working hours. Again, they're proud of their products and genuinely want their customers to enjoy the delicacies they prepare, and it shows.

The moment you stand at the counter, wondering what to buy, (everything smells so good), even if the guy behind the counter is busy attending to another customer he will immediately take the effort to acknowledge your presence at the counter with a smile, a nod and a cheery greeting.

Then he will come to you and tell you what their speciality is.

They actually fill a plateful of different varieties of biscuits, cheese straws, thick slices of cake and give you to taste. And these are all generous helpings. And they do it for all who walk up to their shop.

No **'targeting or segmenting or discriminating'** only those who they think will buy. And they do it for each customer every time he comes, not just the first time, but every time to 'taste'. They're so proud of their products.

"Have the biscuits improved today?", they'll ask a regular customer. "We tried these different ingredients today." They take his feedback. In short, **for them the customer matters, maximum, uppermost.**

"They give such a big piece of cake or such a big biscuit that I feel bad about taking such an expensive piece for trial free, and I try to break off a small piece and have that."

"No no," they say. "Please have the full piece. Then only you'll get the right taste."

If there are four friends who have gone to the shop together and it's obvious that only one of them is buying, the shop attendants will still insist that all four try everything.

Even the most expensive items which you clearly don't intend to buy, they will literally force you to try.

> *Make serving the customer an obsession.*
> - Dr. R. L. Qualls, President & CEO,
>   Baldor Electric Co.

"This is Badampaak, a rich sweetmeat made from the most expensive ingredients like almonds, etc. We're proud of it. It's our speciality. Full of rich ingredients. We only make it in the winter as it's so heavy to digest. Please have a big spoonful. We want your opinion. You'll be doing us a favour. No need to buy. Just try." That's what I was told and given a saucerful of expensive Badampak to taste.

"I literally feel as though I've had a full and free meal when I leave their shop. In fact my wife forbids me from even visiting that shop as even if I don't buy anything, I must be consuming a minimum of 1000 calories on every trip there.

And all this is not a pseudo attempt at CRM or just a show.

We've been around long enough and seen enough to be able to identify the real thing when we see it, even though we see it so rarely.

And believe me, this is the real thing.

They're also very knowledgeable about the ingredients they use, the way they're made, and the final products.

They'll happily and in detail explain to you the difference between whole wheat and maida, between vegetable fat and animal fat, the benefits each gives and so on.

As I said, they're not at all stingy about the pieces they offer to taste.

In fact if a broken biscuit has come onto the sample plate by mistake, they'll apologise, immediately lift it off before you can take it and make sure you have only an unbroken one.

I feel so good when I visit that bakery. I look forward to visit there. In fact you know how it is with places you hate to go to, you tend to finish off your work there as soon as possible and the places you like, you keep to the end, to relish.

Like on my dinner plate, I always keep the jumbo prawns till the end so I can savour them at my leisure.

The same way when I have to visit the area where Paris Bakery is located, I always finish all my other work first and leave my visit to Paris Bakery till the end, like a special treat.

I wonder how many organisations can have that sort of positive impact on their customers.

You know how going to some places is like a dreaded task. You anticipate there'll be some problem because of your past experience, and there usually is.

Here, it's the opposite. I'm all set for a happy experience. And they make sure I always get it," ended Harsh.

"Hey, I can vouch for that if you're talking of the Paris Bakery at Marine Lines," said Radhika. "It's run by this real gentleman called Danesh. I've always had a fantastic experience there myself. One is, yes, he definitely reserves anything you want and keeps it for you. He was speaking with me the other day when I told him that very few bakeries provide this service and his philosophy is very clear. **He says biscuits and cakes are available on every street in the city. I'm proud you think my biscuits and cakes are so good that they're worth reserving. When you request me to reserve some stuff for you, you're actually doing me a favour by being loyal to my shop. Of course, I'll reserve it for you. It's the least I can do. I realise that all my customers have busy schedules and are not hanging around for me to finish my baking and open the oven. It's my duty to make life easy for the customer. What's the big deal if I have to keep something aside for someone? And you don't need to pay any advance either."**

"Another thing I observed there," continued Radhika, "was that even after I'd made a purchase and paid the bill and if I changed my mind and wanted to exchange what I'd purchased for something else, he would willingly do it and do it even a second and third and fourth time without any sign of irritation. This is so unlike many shops that refuse to exchange even once. Once again it's Danesh's fantastic philosophy at work."

"I remember Danesh saying - **'People have every right to change their minds.'** When they leave the shop I want them to feel thoroughly satisfied with what they've bought and if there's any effort I can put from my side to help the customer feel that way, I'll do it. I've even had people taking stuff home and coming later to ask for an exchange. There I have to regretfully refuse and I explain politely to them that legally no one is allowed to take back food stuffs which have left the shop as there could be a possibility of contamination."

"Some people do get upset even with that but I have instructed all my staff never to argue or be arrogant or lose their temper with a customer; however much they feel they're being provoked. If my staff are starting to feel that way I have told them to go back inside the shop, have a break and cool off and let some other staff take over the handling of that customer. But I have instructed them that if they get into a fight with any customer, for whatever reason, the next day they're out of a job."

"There was this one occasion when I had gone to his bakery," continued Radhika, "and I was carrying with me three books in my hand. Courtesy the good stuff that he stocks I went on a buying spree. Now my hands were full with two large carry bags of bakery goods. I was about to ask him for a carry bag for the books which would make it convenient for me to carry the books when Danesh himself noticed my discomfort. Gently taking the books from my hand, he asked his man to put the books in a plastic carry bag for me. His man did so. Then he himself again looked at the packet and told his man to double it up, to use a second bag to hold the first."

He looked at me and explained. "Although I use the best quality and toughest bags, books tend to have a sharp edge which sometimes cut through the toughest carry bag. It's safer to have a double."

"This gesture of his really floored me. After all the fuss that other shops make about giving a carry bag to carry even their *own* products, this guy gives not one but two, good quality bags to hold books which he has never sold. And he does all this without my even asking. *He has truly put himself in my place and empathised with me. I love this man.*"

"And you know what? **His gestures send across a very strong quality signal to me as well.**"

> *Quality is remembered long after the price is forgotten.*
>   - Gucci Family Motto

"If he's so generous and open hearted with plastic bags, which admittedly have a cost attached to them, I'm sure that he's using absolutely the best possible ingredients to make his products. For me, this gesture of his of being generous with plastic bags is the ultimate guarantee of quality," exclaimed Radhika.

"And another thing. *His plastic bags have not even the slightest, smallest name of his shop printed on them.* It's an opportunity for free publicity and advertising which too he has shunned. **On one side of the bags is printed the message, 'Thank You, Do come again,' and on the other side is printed the message, 'Please Conserve Electricity.'** Nowhere does the name of his shop appear."

"It requires a gem of a man to not take the advantage of advertising on space which is rightfully his."

"I would trust any business this man started, even if tomorrow he decided to sell computers or mobile phones, Danesh of Paris Bakery would be my first choice."

> *I believe you have attained customer satisfaction when customers return to your store because they want to, not because they have to.*
>
> - Richard T. Takata, President & COO, Eagle Hardware & Garden Inc.

"Their attitude is so generous; one gets the feeling that if they were in the jewellery business, they'd be giving small pieces of gold away as free samples. Really."

"But what I remember the best is that one leisurely day when I had an interaction with him in his shop," continued Radhika. "I asked Danesh a few questions as I was eager to learn more about his excellent philosophy of customer relations.

I really wanted to understand why and how he was so different from most of the similar shops I had visited. I asked Danesh if he could spare some time for a chat.

"Sure," he said, ever smiling and willing.

I first asked him how old the establishment was.

"More than 50 years old," was his reply.

I had asked this question merely to see if his generous philosophy was practical and profitable over a period of time. It definitely was. **50 years** is more than enough time to judge whether something works or not.

Then I asked him about his philosophy of handing out free samples of everything for every customer to taste, literally forcing them to taste a goodie even if they politely refused.

"Doesn't this generous attitude eat into your profits?", I asked.

"Let me tell you something," said Danesh. **"Sample is the Secret of Business.** Most businesses today behave penny wise and pound foolish. You understand what I'm saying? They always think of what they're going to **GET**. First you **GIVE** and then you get much more than you could have expected. That's why I call samples the secret of good business. I am so confident of the taste and quality of my products, that very many customers after tasting, immediately buy something they liked. Even if they say they don't want to buy and therefore don't want to taste, I have no problem. Just taste, I tell them. Give me a report. Give me your feedback. I get great pleasure out of letting people know that this quality exists in the market. They taste. Even if they don't buy immediately, five days later the taste hits them, they think of me, and come back. It happens almost every time."

> *Golden Rule of Business – "All other things being equal, people will do business with and refer business to only those people they know, like and trust."*
>
> - Cyrus M. Gonda & Kalim Khan

Then I told him, "Fine. I get your point about tasting. But even in the few places which I have seen that do give out free samples, they give pieces of biscuits that have been broken while baking and which anyway they wouldn't have been able to sell. If it's only the taste that you want people to get, why give them the full biscuits? I notice that you only keep boxes of whole biscuits for sampling and you're so generous that when I come away from your shop, I feel I've had a full meal. You use the best quality ingredients as well. Doesn't this eat into your cost?"

"Let me answer that," he said. "I give whole biscuits for two reasons. One, what impression does it give about me if I give broken pieces to my valuable customers?"

"And second and more important, what respect am I showing my most valued customers if I give them broken biscuits to cat? Are they dogs?"

"Let me tell you something. **No businessman makes a loss.** Everything is accounted for when a businessman does his costing."

> *The man who will use his skill and constructive imagination to find out how MUCH he can give for a dollar instead of how LITTLE he can give for a dollar, is bound to succeed.*
>
> - Henry Ford

"The problem with some service providers, is even **after** including these things in their costing and doing the pricing accordingly, they are still so stingy and short sighted that they don't wish to part with something that is already accounted for."

"Let me give you an example," Danesh continued. "The other day I was at a leading international fast food chain, having a sandwich, when I heard an uproar at the cash counter. The place was packed and the lady customer creating the commotion was so upset and so loud that everyone in the place started staring there to see what the problem was. Everyone soon knew because she was yelling so loudly. It seems she had ordered a burger and wanted mayonnaise with the burger. Now in most small, family run fast food joints, mayonnaise is already a part of the burger. But not here. Here it's apparently considered an **extra** and you have to pay separately for it. Fine. But after paying Rs.15 as an extra, what she got was a small spoonful of mayonnaise which couldn't have cost the fast food joint more than 2 rupees as a cost, and for this they were charging the customer Rs.15 extra. Being in the food business myself, I felt bad for the lady. She was saying that this much mayonnaise was not enough for her and that she wanted more. **The manager was telling her you can't have more, you can have extra.** By which he meant, pay another Rs.15 and get another spoonful. She said that 15 bucks was anyway too much for just a spoonful and I agreed with her whole heartedly. She'd already paid Rs.15 extra and wanted more mayonnaise to her satisfaction without paying anything still further for it. She was right. That would have meant paying Rs.30 for just 2 spoonfuls of mayonnaise. Ridiculous. I agreed with her. The manager was equally adamant saying this was their policy and system and she'd have to pay if she wanted extra mayonnaise and there was nothing like more mayonnaise that he was allowed to provide."

> *Quality in a Product or Service is not what you put into it, it's what the customer gets out of it.*
>
>   - Peter Drucker

"The other staff had also left their work and had moved closer to observe what was going on. Customers were left unattended. Everyone was listening intently."

Danesh continued, "That's when I couldn't control myself, I got up, went to the manager, took him aside, and told him 'You call yourself a manager? You're supposed to take decisions. You represent an international fast food chain, **which spends millions on advertising, and you're creating a racket over a spoonful of mayonnaise?** She's already paid 15 bucks for extra mayonnaise and she's not satisfied with what she got for her money. Screw your procedure and system. **What system tells a world wide organisation to fight with a paying customer over a spoonful of mayonnaise?** She's not asking for gold. **Can't you see the damage in terms of reputation it's costing you?** It's not that just because you give her a little more mayonnaise everybody's going to ask for the same. If you'd given it to her when she asked for it first no one would have known. And what's it costing you?'

Finally good sense prevailed and he gave her more mayonnaise. But I can't believe these guys. I'm not saying let people take advantage of you and give away the shop. No way. That's not what I'm advocating. If someone comes daily to my shop and keeps on asking for samples of everything to taste and doesn't buy, I'll politely tell him that he's already sampled everything I have to offer. But you should be able to differentiate a genuine customer from someone who's trying to take advantage of you. I believe you have to give the customer the benefit of the doubt until you're sure of his intentions."

Customers are satisfied when they get what they expect, both with regards to results and behaviour. Creating satisfied customers requires that expectations about performances and about the nature of the relationship be managed and met. We have satisfied customers because we get the job done and because we are responsive.

- James E. Cayne, President & CEO,
Bear Stearns & Co. Inc.

"That's really insightful," I told Danesh. "I have one more question for you. I've observed that most store guys are very possessive and stingy when it comes to plastic bags. I've noticed that you are very generous in this regard as well. What's your take on that?"

"Danesh then proceeded to give me some of **the best customer service insights and lessons I had ever heard or will hear.**"

> *Here is a simple but powerful rule, always give people more than they expect to get.*
>
> - Nelson Boswell

"My logic is simple," said Danesh. "When the customer buys any product at my store, he's spending his hard earned money. When he does that it's my responsibility to see that my product reaches his house in perfect condition. After that it's upon the customer. But the least I can do is ensure that my packaging gives him no problem on the way home.

If someone requests that they've to take the stuff outstation, I even pack it in a nice box at no extra charge. I can empathise with customers who want a good strong plastic bag for carrying the goods home as a few times I myself have suffered for the same reason being a customer at other places. For example there's this dairy a little way from my place which sells the most fantastic curd you've ever had. But the owner is so stingy he never gives you a carry bag. Twice I've taken the curd and because I've had to hold the packet in the palm of my hand and obviously it's wet and slippery and greasy, it's fallen splat on the ground and that's the end of it. **I feel so upset that someone can make such a fantastic product and then be so narrow minded and short sighted not to give a good carry bag.**

My philosophy is not one of **'Khel Khatam and Paisa Hajam.'** Which translates as **Take the money and the show is over.** No. That is not my style.

I am with the customer right till the moment my products reach his place."

"The other day," Danesh went on, "I bought more than 500 rupees worth of groceries from a shop and he gave me such a thin plastic bag that I was sure it would tear on the way.

I asked him for a double bag and he said, "No, No. One bag is enough. It won't break."

"And as was bound to happen (the bag being so thin), five minutes away from the shop, the handle tore away and all the groceries were all over the road. I was so disgusted I decided to black list that shop permanently. And I purchase quite a lot of raw material for my own bakery. I was just trying out that shop for the first time and it was the last. So I know what the customer feels and what he goes through and I do my best to ensure that my customers don't have to face the type of incidents I have suffered. And as I said, I've considered the cost of the bags in my costing so it's a win-win situation."

"It is not that the shops which refused to provide the plastic bags did so out of any environmental concern. They did it just to save a buck at the cost of losing valuable customers."

> *Plastic bags are a euphemism for any small thing not even worth 1% of product value for which an unpleasant taste is created. Customers buy cakes and sweetmeats to sweeten the mouth, but with these incidents, end up getting a bitter taste. Do you think they'll come back?*
>
> *Think small rather than big in the sense if you focus on the so called small things; the nitty gritty, the big things take care of themselves. No matter how large your goal is, it's the small details that ensure your success. Each industry has its own unique 'plastic bag', which if not focused upon or ignored is an irritant, like a small toothache which forces the body to focus its entire attention on it.*
>
> — Cyrus M. Gonda & Kalim Khan

"Wow. Was all that I could say," exclaimed Radhika. "A few more guys like Danesh around in the service business and the better we all would be served. I have become a fan of this guy and whenever I get an opportunity I recommend him to anyone. Although I stay at the other end of the city from where his bakery is located I still make it a point to go there regularly and each time the experience only improves like fine wine which grows better with age. I would salute him as one of the best service people around and as far as his customers are concerned he would win any award for **Caring Customer Service.**"

8

The Air Care

"Cheers to men like Danesh of Paris Bakery," said Furqan.

"Hey, this is getting really interesting. Anyone got any more Ketchups to add to the conversation?", said Rashi waving the Ketchup bottle like a coveted trophy.

"I think we should trademark the word Ketchup... Sounds interesting," chipped in Harsh.

Everyone started talking at once. Obviously there were tons, or rather gallons of Ketchups which had affected everyone's lives one way or the other and they were all eager to share them.

After all, at the end of the day, when cricket heros and Bollywood Zeros have been discussed, people do want to talk about and share the experiences they have had with their service providers who form such an important part of their lives.

That's why Word Of Mouth Publicity has become such an important way for any business to promote itself. Come to think about it, our lives today center around our service providers, so it's but natural that they come to dominate our conversations.

The list of service providers we interact with daily is mind boggling.

"You have to listen to this. I will not let anybody speak," insisted Sunil.

"Oh gosh, you are bossing again… old habits die hard," commented Ushma.

"You guys talked about a Resort, Bakeries and Sweetmeat shops. I want to share my experience about the airline Nice Flight with whom I just flew to Kolkota last week. You know I travel frequently…"

"Now you've started blowing your own trumpet again," chuckled Rashi.

"Shut up yaar. You have to listen to this. This is the ultimate Ketchup. Coming to the point, this air service Nice Flight, in all it's advertisements always boasts about it's well-trained staff and 'Top Shot' Service. I was on a short business trip, out one evening and back the next. You all know I'm very particular and I had given all my preferences when I took the ticket. As it was an evening flight, and one of the longest domestic sectors, Mumbai-Kolkata, which is even longer than Mumbai-Dubai, obviously there would be dinner served on the flight. As usual I gave my preference as Non-Vegetarian.

In spite of leaving home well on time, I got stuck in a traffic jam and was delayed. I was the last passenger to board the plane just in time for takeoff.

I was trying my hardest to shove my laptop into the overhead rack and was finding it very difficult to do so. Considering the fact that I'm so short, that's only natural.

Instead of coming to my assistance, the air-hostess literally yelled at me all across the plane, making me go back to my kindergarten days and think of my KG teacher, Mrs. Fernandes.

"First of all you're late. And now you're fiddling with the baggage rack. Kindly sit down," she said quite rudely.

> *The tongue has a power to hurt. Also to heal. Be careful of every word you speak. It can affect many lives – INCLUDING YOUR OWN.*
>
> - Sadhu Vaswani

Maybe their training programs for this top shot service had been devised by Adolf Hitler.

Thoroughly intimidated, I sat down. Luckily the passenger next to me, who was a tall guy, helped me out with my laptop.

The flight took off, and as is my habit, I asked for a blank paper to pen my thoughts and utilise my time.

Then I was gifted one of the biggest bottles of ketchup you could imagine.

"I am sorry, Sir, we don't have any blank paper onboard this flight."

WHAAAAAAAAAAT ?????

"I said I'm sorry Sir, we don't have any blank paper on board this flight," she slowly repeated as if explaining something very simple to a small child. And then off she went to attend to presumably more important tasks.

I stared after her as she walked down the aisle, popping my ears with my fingers to ensure that I had heard her correctly and that it wasn't the effect of the pressurized cabin on my eardrums.

The guy seated next to me nodded sympathetically. He would have made a better cabin crew. Maybe he had received his training at a better place.

"Yup, you heard right," he said. "They don't have any blank paper, man. But if you want some, here." He opened his briefcase and handed me a couple of sheets of blank paper.

I thanked him and started to write. The first thing which came to my mind and which I wrote down was this incident of sheer and utter unpreparedness on behalf of the airline in not even carrying blank sheets of paper for passengers to use.

I didn't think I had made such an unreasonable request. After all, my neighbour provided me with what actually should have been the airline's responsibility.

I wondered what else to write down when I finished that, but I need not have worried. The airline staff was hell bent on providing me juicy material to write. There was more to come before we landed. Plenty more.

Dinner service commenced and the food trolleys started coming down the aisle from both sides.

As my seat was in the middle of the plane, I would probably be one of the last ones to be served. Never mind, I was pretty hungry and the longer the wait, the more I would relish the meal.

I wondered what dinner would be as I salivated.

Butter chicken, or perhaps fish curry more likely since we were on the way to Kolkota.

Either chicken or fish, any one of them would be just fine, I thought to myself.

The trolley from the front reached me just as the trolley from the back reached the seat behind me. As I had expected I was going to be the last to be served. That was fine by me but what I didn't anticipate was that I'd be served a bottle of ketchup, giant size. No, not served, that's not the right word, more accurately. I was banged over the head with it.

"VEG or NON-VEG, Sir," came the standard question. Actually if they wanted to provide a good experience, they didn't need to ask this question. The information was clearly provided by me at the time of making the reservation, and a little effort on their side would have ensured that they would have known which passenger had ordered what, and could have served my preference without asking me. My respect for their "Top Shot Service" would have gone up.

But that's obviously too much to expect when they are only promising top shot service. I guess they yet have to graduate to world class standards.

"Non-Veg please," I said, emphasizing the 'please'. (SHE hadn't said PLEASE while asking me my preference).

Just because they seemed to have forgotten their manners was no reason for me to do the same.

Now, the ketchup.

"I'm sorry, sir, but we're out of Non-Veg. Can I serve you the Veg option? The Veg option is quite good," she added, obviously intending to pacify me before I threw a tantrum like a small child who has his lollipop snatched away from him.

I wasn't about to fall for that line of flawed reasoning.

"But didn't you just ask me my preference?", I asked, making a tremendous effort to keep my cool.

"I did sir, but that's just S.O.P."

"What do you mean, S.O.P.?"

"S.O.P. stands for Standard Operating Procedure, Sir. It's a routine question we ask everyone. We are supposed to. We've been trained that way," she added by way of explanation.

Now I was sure that their training programme had been devised by a lunatic.

"You mean to tell me, even though you don't have an option available you still ask me my preference? And this is routine? Are you a sadist?"

"I'm sorry, Sir, please don't make a big deal out of it."

"Big deal? You bet I'll make a big deal. This is ridiculous. And your ads say your service has improved. God help the poor passengers who flew your airline before it improved."

"I'd clearly ordered a Non-Veg meal. My organisation is a registered frequent flyer with your airline, though God knows why. I can understand that you're out of Non-Veg, that happens pretty often, although why that should also happen is a mystery to me. But that I could understand and I'd have taken the Veg food if you'd said so."

"But here, you ask me my preference, and when I tell it to you, you immediately tell me it's not available? And then you have the nerve to tell me I'm making a big deal?"

"I wonder about the training your pilots must have received at this rate."

"What do you want us to do, Sir?", she asked in a bored tone as if this were a daily occurrence for her. "**Routine,**" as she would put it.

I guess it must have been a daily affair.

"I don't want the Veg meal," I said.

"Since you don't have Non-Veg available now, and since you asked me whether I wanted Non-Veg, (You gave me the option, remember?), I won't eat now, I can wait," I added.

"When we land, you can go and get me a Non-Veg meal. I'll eat it here itself, and only then leave the plane."

The guy next to me laughed. "Right on, man. They need a wake-up call. They always do this with someone or the other and get away with it because no one wants to make a scene, and they take advantage of that. If more people stood up for their rights, maybe we'd actually get to see this Top Shot Service in action instead of only hearing about it in advertisements."

"But sir, you can't do that," said the hostess.

"Oh, can't I? Then you don't know me well. I'm from the Press and believe me that's exactly what I'm going to do."

Maybe the word Press did the trick. Within the next 5 minutes a Non-Veg meal (chicken), was magically produced and served to me.

I wondered where it had come from as I'm certain that chickens don't fly as high in the sky as an airplane so she couldn't have plucked it from the sky.

As she had clearly and categorically told me that there were no Non-Veg meals left, I was naturally curious to know where this one had come from. Maybe it was their share. Well, they could always have the Veg meal she had offered me. As she herself had told me the Veg option was "quite good." So they shouldn't have a problem.

I asked her where this chicken meal had come from all of a sudden.

She told me that a passenger in the front row had kindly given up his Non-Veg meal on being requested by her.

I said, "Very noble, could you tell me which passenger it was who has performed such a chivalrous deed, that too for a stranger?"

"Why do you want to know?", she asked.

"I am by nature a polite man," I said. "And I would naturally like to thank the man who has so kindly sacrificed his meal for me. I insist that I thank him before I start to eat."

Seeing that I was very serious about this she tossed her head irritably and said, "If you really want to know, this is a meal which we had kept aside for emergencies, you've got what you wanted, right? Now why don't you have it," and she walked off, thoroughly embarrassed, knowing she was caught on the wrong foot, but too proud to apologise.

> **Pride is the most worthwhile thing to swallow. It is the only thing which when swallowed, never chokes.**
>
> — Sadhu Vaswani

"Not the done thing ma'am. **As a service person, Rule Number 1 is to own up to your mistakes.** Leave your pride at the cabin door. That ought to be drilled in during training. This is basic. **And when management is recruiting people for the post of cabin crew, going for model looks is fine, but priority should be to select people friendly persons.** The best airlines and the best hotel chains internationally spend maximum time in their recruitment process focussing on this aspect, and only once they're certain about this, do they then proceed to verify the technical competence of the candidate.

In fact, a few international air carriers invite their regular passengers to sit on the interview panel at selection time for cabin crew and let them conduct the bulk of the interview as they can best identify the necessary traits they would want in a person serving them. Put them through various situations, demands, check their humility, willingness to serve and go out of the way, etc. Of course the passengers who do so are adequately compensated for their efforts. **If the top management really cared about service they would adopt these measures instead of merely looking for the best spot in town for hoardings to publicise their exaggerated claims."**

> *As far as customers are concerned, YOU ARE THE COMPANY. This is not a burden, but the core of your job. You hold in your hands the power to keep customers coming back – PERHAPS EVEN THE POWER TO MAKE OR BREAK THE COMPANY.*
>
> - Anon

"Top Shot Service?", Hah.

"Well," asked Ushma, "Why do you think she did not serve you the Non-Veg in the first place and avoid all the problems?"

"Who knows what goes on in their warped minds?", said Sunil.

"Maybe they had kept the extra food for themselves to have on the flight or take it home with them for their dinner. I've even heard that the airline tells them to serve as few Non-Veg meals as possible because they can return the ones that are left over and get a refund."

"That may not be true but you see what happens when you

lie once. The customer loses faith and then starts to doubt everything that you say."

It becomes like the story of the **Boy Who Cried Wolf.** You remember that story, right? The boy is always fooling around calling for help saying that the wolf has come to attack him. Every time people come to help him and then realise that he is lying. He **builds a reputation for himself of being a liar.** When the wolf actually comes to attack him and the boy really shouts for help because he needs it, no one turns up thinking that he is lying again. **People would have wanted to help and believe him but his own past record goes against him. The same is true in the case of these organisations.**

One negative incident of this sort can create all sorts of negative impressions in the mind of a valued customer.

This is important for any customer oriented management to remember.

"After all, the concept of MOMENTS OF TRUTH initiated in the Airline Industry," concluded Sunil.

"Since we are talking Airlines, let me share the Ketchup poured on me on my flight back from Bhopal last month," said Rahul, excitedly.

"You guys know I'm terrified of flying. I literally have a phobia about it. Even if it's a long distance trip from Mumbai to Delhi or Bangalore I always take a train.

Last month I had an urgent trip to make to Bhopal and the return train tickets were not available. Anyway I said to myself that it would be a good forced opportunity to get over my phobia, as I've always wanted to travel abroad but this phobia keeps me back. I thought to myself that if I have one pleasant flight experience, I could get over my nervousness. So I booked an 8.30 p.m. flight from Bhopal to Mumbai on Posh Airlines, which incidentally was the last flight of the day from that airport.

As soon as I reached the airport by 7, well before reporting time, as I wanted to get comfortable with the surroundings, I started to get the jitters.

I took my boarding pass and prayed that the flight would be on time.

It wasn't.

That's okay. I can understand that. **What put me off was that they were so callous in their communication, or rather, lack of communication.** As if a couple of hours here and there is all in the game.

Did I say a couple of hours?

Sorry, that's just a figure of expression.

The damn flight was 5 hours late.

All the passengers were bunched up in the departure lounge by 8.15, and then the airline staff decided that the aircraft wasn't fit enough to fly. **As usual, the standard "technical fault" was the scapegoat.**

Every 15 minutes **WE** had to keep asking the airline staff (that is when we could manage to locate one), how long before the flight would take off.

"We're not sure whether it will take off at all," said the only airline staff around, who ironically although his name tag mentioned his name as 'Hasmukh'(which in Hindi means 'Smiling Face'), had a face which looked like it could burst into tears any moment.

At forty five minutes past midnight, when we'd given up all hope of the flight taking off at all, we were suddenly rushed into the flight like cattle, with the crew in an almighty hurry, as if trying to make up for lost time. Unfortunately although the delay hadn't been our fault, we were the ones being rudely hurried.

"Do you need to use the washroom just at this moment?", an angry stewardess asked an elderly lady, who had held back from going to the washroom for the past 4 hours as she'd been afraid she'd miss her flight, as no information had been forthcoming.

When you start viewing your customers as interruptions, you are going to have problems.

- Kate Zabriskie

While I was boarding the bus that takes the passengers to the aircraft, the ground staff stopped me saying that the tag on my laptop bag had not been stamped by security clearance. She was rude to the core and asked me why I hadn't got it done. By now I had lost my patience and bluntly asked her whose fault it was in the first place. I had given my laptop along with other luggage at the security check counter and if the staff there forgets to do the necessary formalities like checking the luggage and sticking their label, I am not to be blamed. In fact I was so furious that I challenged her to prevent me from boarding the plane. The funny part is when I lost my cool the lady just stepped aside and let me board the bus. **The question is what security are we talking of when if a passenger yells, he's allowed to bypass security procedures. That means that the check was not mandatory in the first place.**

Well, we all were seated in the plane and my jitters were now at fever pitch. The plane took off and I felt I needed something to calm my nerves and occupy my time.

Luckily there was an in flight magazine on the seat which had a crossword puzzle which looked as if it could occupy my time nicely through the fifty minute flight.

Immediately after take off I asked the steward for a pen so that I could absorb my mind in the crossword puzzle and not think about the flight. The person next to me had a severe headache, apparently from waiting so long and requested the steward for a headache pill.

"Yes Sir, yes Sir, three bags full," was the polite answer from the steward every time he passed us and we reminded him about our requirements.

I counted at least five times during the forty minutes flight (excluding five minutes each for take off and landing), that we requested him, me for the pen and my co-passenger for his headache pill.

At last, just as we were about to put on our seat belts prior to landing, success, but only for me. I got the pen, at least I managed to hurriedly scribble one solution in my crossword before I had to put on the seat belt for landing.

My co-passenger never did get his pill, but ironically we both did get our Namaste, the traditional Indian greeting, from the stewardess as we got off the plane, and a **mugged up parroted greeting, hoping we had a pleasant flight and would we please fly this airline again.**

High hopes.

"That's my Ketchup, and rather than soothing my phobia of flying, they did a good job of zooming up my phobia of flying sky high," concluded Rahul munching the kebabs.

> *Unless you have 100% customer satisfaction,*
> *YOU MUST IMPROVE.*
> - Horst Schulz, COO, Ritz Carlton Hotels

"What you guys experienced was bad service. But what I went through was not only bad service but disgusting attitude and an intolerable insult," jumped in Ushma, as if she was waiting for Rahul to conclude. "I am sure you would like to hit that creep once you get to know how he behaved with me. I can't wait to tell you guys."

"Oh my God, somebody could actually misbehave with you... anyways, continue," said Farah.

"Since we are talking about airlines, you GOT to listen to what happened to me." continued Ushma. "You know I travel a lot abroad for work with my office colleagues and many times alone. I was traveling with a group of 5 female colleagues to Cairo by this prominent International Airlines. Our group was trying out this Airline for the first time as their advertisements promised excellent care and service. The flight was packed and our group was scattered all over the plane. **I didn't get a window seat which I had specifically requested for and had been assured about by the reservation staff, but that's understandable as the plane was full.**

Unfortunately, I was seated next to a guy who leered at me as soon as I sat down. I already felt uncomfortable and I had a long flight ahead. But then, you can't blame a guy for just staring.

I started to read a magazine. I could feel the arm of the guy next to me starting to touch mine on the seat-rest. I moved my arm slightly away. A minute later his arm followed mine and increased the pressure. He also started to incline his head on my side, almost resting on my shoulder. Now I was feeling thoroughly unconfortable and I still had a long flight ahead of me.

I didn't want to create a scene so I just got up and walked down the aisle to the steward and quietly told him what the problem was. I spoke softly as I didn't want anyone else or the guy who was misbehaving to hear me. I just wanted to change my seat. The steward told me to follow him and I did so, thinking he was escorting me to another seat somewhere which was vacant. **He stopped exactly at the spot where I had been seated and loudly asked me so that everyone in the range of 5 rows could hear."**

"Is this the seat where you are having a problem?"

This is exactly what I had wanted to avoid. I could see that guy staring at us now with the dirty smile still on his face.

"Yes," I said softly. By now I was thoroughly embarrassed although it hadn't been my fault at all.

"Well," said the steward to me, casually glancing around the plane. "You can see as well as I can that the flight is full. There is not a single empty seat where I can seat you. **I guess our airline is doing very well. Everyone wants to travel with us." And he laughed at his own stupid joke.**

By now all the passengers nearby were also starting to stare. My entire group was scattered far away and they weren't aware what was going on.

"Can't you request some male passenger to change seats with me," I mumbled, looking shame-facedly down at the carpet.

"I can't do that," he said. "You could ask around and see if someone is willing to change seats with you. I have to serve snacks to all the passengers. They are waiting." And he walked off, leaving me in an even worse state than before, totally at the mercy of the guy next to me. I couldn't obviously sit there now nor did I feel like asking a stranger nearby for a favour.

This obviously highly paid airline steward, representing an International airline, didn't care how I was treated by my fellow passenger, **but truly Great Service Orgnisations ensure that no customer is disturbed, upset or harassed by another.**

> *If you must gargle, do it without upsetting the other customers.*
>
> - Sign in a Restaurant,
> (Ideal Corner, Parsi Cuisine, Fort, Mumbai)

Luckily, a young lad seated nearby, who had by now understood the entire episode voluntarily offered to exchange seats and saved me from further embarrassment.

"I can expect passengers behaving like this. It can't be helped," continued Ushma.

"But that steward?"

"His attitude?"

Instead of being sympathetic and respecting my privacy and coming to the assistance of a female passenger who has been badly treated by a co-passenger, he insensitively yells out my complaint in front of that guy's face and then laughs over his own stupid jokes.

> *Common sense is of paramount importance in Business and Customer Service.*
>
> - Anon

Shouldn't the airlines train their staff to empathise and be tactful when handling such delicate situations? And if it is conducting these trainings, is the management following up to ensure that the learnings are put into practice...... and they don't even have a proper system to ensure that one can get redressal in case of a grievance. Inspite of my busy schedule, I visited the office of this airline after the flight to register my grievance. All I was told was to put my complaint in writing and submit it at the counter. No one ever got back to me. I have never flown that Airline again, nor has any one else from my group done so.

We see our customers as guests invited to a party and we are the hosts. It's our job EVERY day to make EVERY important aspect of the customer experience a little better.

- Jeff Bezos

"Ya, these are real shockers and definitely not expected from airlines which advertise and claim high levels of service. I guess this is reality at the grass root level but thankfully I have some positive experiences to narrate about airline service which I have witnessed and observed," said Farah.

"You know I am a frequent traveler but yet it's not very often that I have seen airline staff going out of their way. I definitely have seen it a few times and I wish it were more often. **It would be such a pleasure to fly and if an airline through it's staff consistently gave me such memorable service I would be it's loyal passenger for life.**"

A satisfied customer is the best strategy of all.

- Michael LeBoeuf

An incident I clearly remember as positively outstanding happened a few years back when I was flying Azad Airlines. There was this elderly and partially handicapped lady who was finding it difficult to have her meal by herself. Well I agree that it is the job of the cabin crew to help out such passengers, but in most cases I have seen that these tasks are ignored or passed on by the seniors to the junior most staff and even the junior crew member does it extremely reluctantly, making faces and making it very obvious that it is an unpleasant chore and they try to get it over as soon as possible, literally shoving the food in the person's mouth. **But here I saw the senior airhostess personally handling the task lovingly and gently feeding the elderly lady as if she were her own mother, also personally assisting her to the washroom.**

What else can differentiate one airline from another ?

Here there was **Care, Commitment and Concern** and if these three C's can be attributed to a service person, I say to hell with everything else. Were not the **same three qualities** attributed to **Mother Teresa and Florence Nightingale, and weren't these two ladies the epitome of service ?**

"That's great, that's really touching, that's truly what service should be about," said Rashi.

> *If you work just for money, you will never make it, but if you love what you are doing, success will be yours.*
> - Ray Croc, Founder of McDonald's

"I too witnessed an excellent example of service when I was flying to London by Asia Airlines," said Radhika, "The passenger next to me was airsick and puked and spoilt his shirt and was worried as he immediately had to attend an important business meeting on landing and all his other shirts were packed in the luggage. As soon as he mentioned his problem, a crew member, who overheard, immediately offered him his personal shirt which he was carrying in his kit."

"That is really going out of the way," said Furqan.

"I also have heard of an airline overseas where after the owner received a complaint of very little leg space in the last row, he removed the last row in all planes, letting go that revenue but ensuring a paying customer gets convenience at all times," added Sunil. "For example, in Emirates Airlines, when a passenger asks for water, the crew gives him royal treatment by getting two glasses of water on a tray, one chilled and one normal temperature, he can choose which he prefers. But in another airline I have noticed the steward get a bottle of water with a pile of plastic glasses from which the passenger himself has to pull out a glass, pour water from the bottle and serve himself."

> *You'll never have a product or a price advantage again, they can be easily duplicated. But a strong service culture can never be copied.*
> — Jerry Fritz

"Do you know every commercial airline company in the world either has a Boeing or an Airbus aircraft? There is no other company in the world making heavy commercial aircraft. So every airline has the same planes with more or less the same features and which fly at the same speed as all other airlines. **The only differentiator therefore is their service,**" remarked Apurva.

> *Being on par in terms of price and quality only gets you into the game, service wins the game.*
> — Tony Allessandra

Airlines like Emirates, Swiss and Singapore Airlines don't rate highly with passengers and win awards because their aircraft are superior. They are not. IT'S THEIR SERVICE WHICH MAKES THEM OUTSTANDING AIRLINES.

You will discover that you have two hands. One is for helping yourself and the other is for helping others.

- Audrey Hepburn

What we have done for ourselves alone dies with us; what we have done for others and the world remains and is immortal

- Albert Pike

9

The Mall Misery

"I think we should all thank Apurva for this get together," said Sunil. "Else we could have never got to discuss these Ketchups."

"Yeah, I do all the arrangements and Apurva gets the credit," complained Radhika. "You know I actually went around shopping in a couple of malls to make arrangements for today."

"Malls... Malls... talking of bad service, I think they rule the show," intervened Rahul.

"Tell me about it. I think the more the glamourised the structure of the mall, the more questionable is the service," added Rashi fuming with anger, as if recollecting some horror stories.

"Hey, hey, hey, since we are all talking of these issues, I just got to share something with you guys," burst in Furqan. "It's something I think about so often."

"Not another one on airlines? Even you've been traveling frequently," interrupted Apurva.

"No, no. Although we have just been talking about airlines, the incidents I want to share have nothing to do with aviation. But they are from a Service Industry which is currently being talked about everywhere. **It's Retail.**"

"Hey, should I serve dinner while Furqan serves the Ketchup?", asked Radhika.

"No hurry. Are you trying to drive us out early?", joked Ushma.

"And by the way this Ketchup thing is getting a little too interesting," said Rashi. "It affects us all every day of our lives and affects the buying decisions and relationships we make and strengthen. Let's see what you've got to say, Furqan. And I want to see if your experiences are better or worse than mine."

"Well," went on Furqan, putting his arm around his wife Farah. "You've all seen our little Umar. He's about six now. I'm telling you about something which happened about a couple of years ago. You know how fast kids are growing up nowadays and how tech -savvy they're getting."

"I agree with you in totality," said Sunil. "Whenever I need to get something on the computer done, I tell my son to do it for me. And he's only ten. I feel outdated."

"True. Anyway that's what I'm trying to tell you all about. You know I'm the head of P.R. and Corporate Communications with the Organisation for which I work. We have lots of foreign delegates who come down to Mumbai and I take them around the place, show them the sights, and also take them to do their shopping.

Since they are used to the massive malls abroad, I try to take them to the largest malls we have so they can feel at home. I could take them to any store, they trust my judgment. But since I want to ensure that they have a good experience, I avoided taking them to smaller outlets as I assumed the service and the overall experience would definitely be much better in the larger places. Normally I preferred to take them to this mall, Great Mall in Mumbai.

And believe me, over the years these guys I have taken there have purchased a lot. I must be single-handedly responsible for this mall getting at least 20 lakhs worth of business. And I have never taken any advantage of it like asking for discounts for myself or anything of that nature. I just wanted these delegates to have a good impression of the shopping standards in our city.

Then one day I went to Great Mall myself with Farah to pick up something for Umar as his birthday was coming up.

There were so many options, with all these new computer games and play stations and stuff like that; we were quite confused about what to buy. We finally picked up a computer based game.

The staff in the toy department were pretty vague in their knowledge of the functioning of the various games, but at least they were friendly.

When we selected and bought a game (it cost around 5000 bucks), we asked the staff and cashier that if the game was not suitable for our four year old, in terms of it being too advanced and complicated for him, could we exchange it for something simpler?"

"Yes, you can. Just get the bill and make sure you make the exchange within a week's time from today," answered the cashier monotonously, **without looking up from his computer screen.**

> ***Eye contact is a visual handshake.***
> -Stephen Boyd

"Thanks, we'll keep that in mind," we said. "His birthday is day after tomorrow, and if he can't handle it, or it's too difficult for him, we'll come back within three or four days itself, not later."

As we left the mall, I told my wife, "These guys seem to be getting more customer oriented. Their exchange policies are improving."

"Uh, huh, it's easy to say all this. I'd prefer to see the policy in action," she said, cautious as ever. It turned out she had judged them better than I had. Maybe there is something to this women-being-smarter and more intuitive business after all.

But at that time all I told her was, "Come on, you're just being negative."

"I'm not, I'm just being realistic. I prefer to believe things when I see them happening. **Talk is cheap, in fact it's free.**"

We reached home, played with Umar for a while, and dozed off. The day after that we gave him his gift at his birthday party. He seemed pretty thrilled with the soft toys and the board games that he got but he didn't seem too happy with the electronic games. He'd always been that way and we wanted him to take more interest in high-tech things since that's what his generation is going to grow up with."

"Maybe we just have a late developer on our hands," I told my wife.

"That's all right," she replied. "He's just four. I don't think this computer game we picked up is appropriate for him right now. It's good that we told the guys at the mall that we might come back and exchange it for something more suitable. Tomorrow is a bank holiday. Let's go there tomorrow itself in the evening and then we can go out for an early dinner before the restaurants get packed with the holiday rush. Just pack up the game in it's cardboard box and remember to take the bill along," reminded Farah.

Next evening we reached the mall by around six thinking it would take us a maximum of half an hour to select something else and complete the exchange formalities.

As we reached there, I wanted to go to the washroom. I went there but it was shut for renovation. I was directed to the staff loo which was so packed with yelling employees who pushed me around that I decided to give it a miss. I met my wife and Umar outside the loo where they were waiting for me and started to walk down the staircase to the basement where the toy section was. Umar was walking down holding the wooden railing alongside the staircase.

Suddenly he let out a yell and started crying. I took a quick glance and saw his finger bleeding.

Then I noticed that the glass under the wooden railing he was holding was broken and had jagged edges.

I quickly rushed him to the staff loo and bathed his finger under running water. Luckily it wasn't a deep cut, but it definitely could have been much worse, considering how badly the glass had been broken.

I located a floor manager and asked him for a Band-Aid.

I also asked him how the hell they could allow a broken jagged glass to remain like that over there on the bannister.

"It just broke today morning," was his blunt reply.

"Today morning? And it's now past 6 in the evening." I yelled. "It's a bank holiday. Your mall is packed with holiday crowds, including kids, any one of whom could have cut themselves."

"And what if someone was hemophilic and bled to death? You've had 10 hours to take care of this and you've not even put some white tape over the broken glass so it won't hurt anyone? That's the least you could have done. What kind of people run this place? Are they on drugs?"

"I'm sorry, Sir, I'll get it done right away," said the floor manager apologetically.

"Yeah, sure you will," I thought to myself.

> *The atmosphere and the service in the stores is what determines the customer satisfaction level. It's really the total atmosphere that we give to people in the stores, that we are there to help them and to serve them and make sure their purchase is a good purchase for them.*
> *Once that is executed and executed well nobody can take that away from you. Its your total personality in the retail business that counts and that total execution that makes your business unique.*
> — Gordon I. Seagal, CEO, Crate & Barrel

"You better," I told him. "Lucky it's not too deep a cut. Anyway, can you arrange for a Band-Aid quickly?"

"Sure sir, we have a first-aid box on the ground floor of the mall. I'll send someone down to get a Band-Aid immediately. Please wait right here."

I waited with Farah and Umar, who was still in considerable pain.

We waited for fifteen minutes and then I went to the manager again and asked him what the problem was. "What's going on, man? Fifteen minutes to go down two floors and get a Band-Aid and come up?"

He apparently had forgotten all about it. (I guess anything which is not related to an immediate sale and profit is on the back burner for these guys). He phoned the ground-floor. Presumably that's where the first-aid box was located.

He spoke to someone, mumbled "I see," and put the phone down.

"What's the problem now?", I asked him, seeing that he wasn't going to speak without being asked.

He hesitated and said, "Sir, they are trying to locate the key to the first-aid box. It seems it's misplaced. Shouldn't take more than five minutes."

"I don't believe this," said Farah disgustedly and insisted that we leave.

We had just turned to leave when the manager's phone rang and he picked it up. He had a beaming smile on his face when he put it down.

"They located the key," he said, as excitedly as though they had found a pot of gold.

"Some staff member had kept it in his pocket and gone out for a smoke," he added.

"Spare me the explanations," I said. Just take us down to where the box is; let us fit on the Band-Aid ourselves. We could have left long back if you had told us immediately that the key was misplaced. Anyway, let's go down."

He escorted us down to where the first-aid box was located.

"Well, can I have the Band-Aid please, as you've finally managed to get the box opened."

He stammered again. "Uh, ----- you see Sir, we've opened the box but there are no Band-Aids inside. The person who used them last must have forgotten to re-stock…"

I didn't even wait for him to finish his sentence. I was afraid I would really have lost my temper. I dragged Farah and Umar out with me and we went to a nearby chemist shop, bought a Band-Aid and put it on Umar's finger.

"We'll come back tomorrow, exchange the gift and that's the last I'm seeing of this bloody mall," I told Farah. "I don't think I'll ever get any of my delegates to shop here any more. I don't want any embarassing situations like this involving them."

We had some light snacks outside and went home, our evening ruined by the negligence and lethargy at the mall.

Next day, I carried the game and bill with me in the morning and decided to get it exchanged after work. During the course of the day I mellowed down a bit.

"These things happen," I told myself.

The loo, the broken glass, the missing key, the missing Band-Aids, at that time I didn't think of them as my Ketchups.

Let me give them another chance, I thought to myself. I shouldn't let one bad experience stop me from taking my delegates there for shopping. I'm going to get the gift exchanged today, go home early after that and spend time with the family. I'll return the computer game, and pick up some good books in exchange for it. Umar loves reading so that should be fine. I thought of gifting something to Farah as well.

Thinking these happy thoughts I reached the mall by 5.30, planning to wrap up the exchange fast and give top priority that evening to Farah and Umar.

I wouldn't be able to spend an evening with them again for quite some time as the next day I had a meeting which would go on till late and the day after I was flying off to London for a 10 day office trip.

I parked my car at the mall, picked up the bag containing the game box, the bill was in my wallet, and I reached the children's section after filling an exchange note at the security so I could carry the game inside.

At the toy counter I quickly selected a board game which I thought we could all play together and four nice books which just around made up the price of the game I was returning.

Might as well give Umar some books since he enjoys them. Reading is a great habit at any age. I could always introduce him to computers later, I thought. Look at the state of the world today, needing to be tech savvy at the age of 4. What next, I shook my head and smiled.

I hoped to get this exchange transaction over with in a couple of minutes, get something nice for Farah and rush home before I got hit with the main office traffic. No TV today, it's just the three of us. I had a vision of a pleasant evening spent together before Umar went off to bed by 10. He had early school the next day.

I reached the exchange counter. Luckily there was no line. I handed over the bill and the game box and kept the books and board game ready. I'd already calculated the extra amount I'd have to pay above the previous bill and kept the exact amount ready so as not to waste the slightest time. I still had to pick up Farah's gift as well. That should be from the third floor in the ladies section.

I handed over the computer game as well as the stuff I had picked up in it's place to the lady at the Exchange Counter.

I was about to hand over the cash when I got a rude shock.

A Kingsize bottle of Ketchup right in my face.

"Sorry sir, we can't exchange this."

I stared blankly, her words taking time to register.

"But I was told I could get it back within a week's time if my son was not comfortable with it. It's just been two days and that too I came yesterday itself but we had this stupid mess up because of the broken glass. Then why can't you replace it?", I queried logically.

"Sir, please don't get excited. We can't exchange it because the cardboard box of the game is damaged."

Losers make promises they often break, winners make commitments they always keep.
- Dennis Waitley

I tried to see what she was saying. At last I saw what she was referring to, although it would have helped a lot if I had a magnifying glass to see what she meant. At the lower corner of the box top, there was a tear of about half a centimeter. **How come this eagle eye of theirs goes on vacation when it comes to spotting broken glass and missing keys and Band-Aids I wondered?**

I noticed some similar computer game boxes they had stored on the nearby shelf for sale.

I went up to them and saw that 2 of these boxes were torn far worse than the boxes I was returning.

I hadn't even examined the box carefully when I had first purchased it. The tear she was referring to was so insignificant. And seeing the torn boxes on the shelf I realized that I could easily have been given an already torn box at the time of purchase itself. I told her so.

"I'm sorry Sir; I don't know anything about that. I am not responsible for what is sold. I am only responsible for any exchanges I take back and even if the box is slightly damaged my strict instructions are that I'm not supposed to accept it or I'll be held responsible."

I could see it was no use arguing rationally with her. She had her parrot like speech mugged up and ready and **had clearly been told not to think for herself.** It really wasn't her fault. If the management gave her no autonomy to take decisions and apply her judgement, she couldn't very well do so.

"Can you get me your floor manager," I said, feeling suddenly drained and exhausted.

This mall should be renamed the vampire mall, I thought. It's literally sucking the blood out of me and my family. Yesterday Umar's, physically, and today mine, mentally.

"Sorry Sir, floor manager is off today."

"Then dammit get the floor manager from the floor above."

She made a call while I waited and fumed. In the meantime the exchange desk was packing up with other people coming to exchange their stuff. Poor souls, if only they knew what lay ahead I'm sure they'd have preferred to turn around and leave right then.

I could see my plans for a nice quiet evening with the family going up in smoke. After five minutes she told me, "Sir, floor manager from upper floor has just gone for his break. He'll be back in about twenty minutes."

"Then get the manager from the floor below," I yelled.

She picked up the phone again.

"God, do I have to tell them everything?", I thought.

She put the phone down after talking to someone.

"Well, what's up, has he gone for his break as well?", I asked.

"No sir."

"Then is he coming up?"

"No sir."

"Why not?"

Her answer bowled me over.

"He's gone to attend a Customer Relations Training Programme, Sir. It's a very important programme for all our staff to attend. Our H.R. Department puts great emphasis on attending Customer Service Training Programme, Sir."

I started to count to 10. No, better make it a 100. 10 just wasn't enough for this kind of aggravation.

"Can – You – Get – Me – Someone – Who – Can – Help – Me ..."

I strained out each and every word.

A thirsty guy in a desert couldn't have been more desperate. No one turned up, the lady got immersed in her work and I had no energy left to talk to her again.

After fifteen minutes had passed by the clock on the wall, (I seriously doubted that even the clock worked properly, considering the way everything functioned around here, even the clock would have been spoilt by all the rotten apples around), I went to her again and politely asked, "Do you think the manager would have finished his break by now? Would he mind if we disturbed him?"

"Oh. I'm sorry. I forgot. I'll call him right away."

> **Biggest Question: Isn't it really "Customer Helping" rather than "Customer Service?" And wouldn't you deliver better service if you thought of it that way?**
>
> - Jeffrey Gitomer

A manager came up in another ten minutes, which was much quicker than I expected and I explained the situation to him. By now it was 6.45 and my second evening in a row had been screwed up by these guys.

He heard me out without interrupting, with a bored expression on his face. It appeared he had all the time in the world. I guess he didn't have any evening planned with his family. After I finished he said, "I understand, Sir, but what the lady at the exchange counter said is correct. You see, we have to return any exchanged piece to the manufacturer, **that's our policy**. The manufacturer will thoroughly check it to see if there is any damage to the product or the box and he will not accept such a product as a return from us. If the box was intact, we would have taken it back."

"You know," I told him, "This reminds me of a very appropriate joke. There was this farmer who went to his neighbour to borrow a rope. The neighbour said, "Sorry, I would have lent it to you, but right now I'm using the rope to tie up my milk."

"Tie up your milk? You can't tie up milk with a rope."

"I know that. But when I don't want to do something, one excuse is as good as another."

"If I don't want to do a thing, I can think of a hundred excuses, and if I want to do a thing, I will overcome a hundred obstacles."

"It's not like that, Sir. But we can't take it on our head. We would be responsible and have to pay for it out of our salary if the manufacturer doesn't take it back."

I pointed out the already torn boxes on the shelf for sale.

"I agree sir, but this is different."

How it was different he could never quite explain. Maybe the difference was **according to them it should be buyers beware and not sellers beware.**

Then I blasted. I brought the house down.

"I want to see someone capable of making a sensible decision. Is there anyone of that type here or is this mall orphaned?"

People were staring but I was past caring.

Let them stare, in fact the more the merrier. I wanted them to stare. I wanted them to know the kind of attitude the management displayed towards their GOD, The Customer.

Suddenly, an official looking guy in a suit came rushing over. "What's the problem?", he asked.

"Problems," I said. "The right word is problems. It's not one singular problem. It's plural. It's multiple."

"Starting from your washrooms being out of order, the glass on the staircase cracked and not replaced or repaired, misplaced key of the first-aid box, no Band-Aid inside the box, ridiculous return policy, your manager going on Customer Relation training when there is absolutely no Customer focus at all in reality, miscommunication, stupid excuses, you stocking goods in worse condition for sale than you refuse to accept as return,….." by now I was out of breath.

"Calm down," said the official looking man. He hadn't bothered to introduce himself. "They ARE right, you know, they're just following strict instructions."

"That's exactly the problem," I said. "They're so rigidly following stupid instructions that they've lost the capacity to think sensibly. I don't blame them. I blame the decision makers and the policy framers. Anyway, who are you? I don't think you've introduced yourself."

"I'm the V.P. - Operations of this organization," he explained.

"And I'm the Head P.R. and Corporate Communication with HHL

Ltd. I regularly and repeatedly bring in delegates from India and overseas to shop here and over the past ten years I must have given you guys lakhs worth of business. I realise now what a big mistake I made," I replied.

Hearing this, and seeing my visiting card which I thrust under his nose, his attitude changed.

"Well, I'm sure we can work out something special in your case." He indicated to the girl at the counter that she could go ahead with the exchange.

"I'm not looking for any favours," I said. "This ought not to be a special case. This should be your regular policy. Thanks but no thanks. You can keep your game and the box and I want nothing in return and you'll never be seeing me or my delegates again, but I won't forget you. I'll pass on this incident wherever and to whomever I can."

> *There is only one boss, the Customer, and he can fire everybody in the Company from the Chairman down, simply by spending his money somewhere else.*
>
> - Sam Walton

"You can bet that I forgot to pick up a gift for Farah. By now it was already 8.25. I stormed out.

On the way back I was in a real bad frame of mind as my well planned evening was messed up, I still wanted to be home as soon as possible. I broke a traffic signal, and got a ticket. **Actually, it's a terrific idea. Break a rule, get a ticket, pay a penalty. The day is not far off when customers will have their own official tickets to**

be handed out like red and yellow cards whenever they're the recipients of a bad service. And the authencity of the complaint and the validity of the grievance could be done by the organisation appointing an Ombudsman.

An Ombudsman is an individual with a good public reputation for honesty, who is appointed by an organisation to represent the interest of it's customers by investigating and addressing complaints reported by customers against the organisation.

Appointing an Ombudsman boosts the credibility of an organisation as a concerned service provider sky high, sending across a message that the organisation is serious about service and quality."

> *Every organisation that's serious about providing quality products and services should appoint an ombudsman to establish credibility.*
>
> - Cyrus M. Gonda & Kalim Khan

"I reached home by 9.00 p.m. I was in a foul mood and it showed. Farah and Umar could immediately sense it. After all they'd called me often during the course of the evening to find why I was late inspite of promising to spend the evening with them. Poor things. Guess that mall owes a lot to all of us. Using legal language, it could be termed as Physical Harm, Lethargy, Callousness, Discrimination, Incompetence, Apathy and God knows what else."

> *If the shopper feels it was poor service, then it WAS poor service. We are in the customer perception business.*
>
> - Mark Perrault

"But, now listen to the best part.

A truly fantastic Ketchup.

I mentioned that I went to London the day after this incident in the Great Mall. I finished my business there in about seven days and had a couple of days at the end of the trip reserved for my shopping.

I wanted to buy something for Farah and Umar to make up for what had happened. I picked up some nice perfume for Farah and a silk scarf with a lovely intricate design that I knew she'd like.

Now for Umar. I had to get him to be comfortable with technology. I didn't want him lagging behind his classmates.

I walked into Hamley's, one of the largest speciality toy stores in London. The moment I walked in I was zapped. It looked like Alladin's cave. I started to wish that I were a kid again. Somewhat enviously, I started asking myself why these things hadn't been around when I was at Umar's age.

While I was still soaking in the surroundings, a salesperson politely came up and asked if he could be of help.

Yes, definitely I did need help. I was feeling lost with all this choice around me.

I explained my requirement, told him Umar's age, and that I wanted something basic and simple. He showed me an educational computer game. He was very knowledgeable, and anticipated all my queries, clarified all my doubts in simple language. The game cost 32 pounds. I still recall the exact price.

I was convinced that this would be the right thing for Umar. I told the salesman that I was taking it back to India and could they pack it properly for me? "We sure will, and here is a comprehensive 2 year guarantee which covers all defects. We hope your son will enjoy and learn at the same time. Do visit us again whenever you are in London."

"Thank you." I left truly satisfied. Pleasant, well-trained and knowledgeable staff. Somehow that encounter left me with a lot of faith in their word. No over-promising, just a steady mature assurance.

The flight back from London was uneventful. Landed, rushed home and had dinner with the family after a long time.Farah had made my favourite dishes. After dinner I unpacked my bags and gave Umar and Farah their presents. Farah was thrilled with the perfume. She particularly liked the scarf.

"What did you get for me, Dad?", that was Umar, eager for his gift.

"Here Umar, you'll enjoy this. Be careful, I'll show you how to set it up."

We had dessert and then I tried to set it up exactly as the sales guy in Hamley's had shown me. It didn't work the way it worked there. Maybe I was doing it wrong. None of us are tech-savvy. It's just not in our blood.

I was tired with jet lag. "Umar, we'll try it again tomorrow. Don't be disappointed. You waited so long already. You just need to wait a day longer."

"Okay, dad, no problem," Umar was as calm as ever. That trait of his I'm sure is not passed on from me. That was the good thing about him. That's one good thing he's got from Farah's side of the family.

The next day, I carried the Instruction Manual of the game to work and at lunchtime went through it carefully and also checked with a couple of guys in the IT Department of our office about some points I didn't understand. By the end of lunch hour I thought I'd fairly mastered it. I felt proud of myself. Imagine, a grown man feeling proud about mastering a game meant for a 4 year old.

I went home that evening, had a nice hot tomato soup and sat down with the game with Umar by my side, patiently looking on. I fiddled with it for half an hour, repeating the installation steps over and over again mechanically. No go.

There was something wrong with the machine. "All these people are the bloody same," I muttered. "Got this thing all the way from London. Worked well in the shop and now as soon as I reach home….."

"I'm sorry, Umar, guess we both have no luck with anything electronic. Anyway, they've given an e-mail address on their bill. Let me mail and see if they respond. I doubt I'll even get a reply. After all, if this is how the mall in my own city, to whom I've given lakhs worth of business, treated me, how can I expect a positive response from the other side of the world.

But I had nothing to lose. I decided to mail them from office the next day.

I reached office, opened my mail, and before I sent them a stinker, I read my incoming mail for the day. Among the other mail I received was a mail from Hamley's, thanking me for patronising their store, hoping I was enjoying the gift I had purchased. (They mentioned the specific game I had bought, so it wasn't a standard letter, it was at least customised), and ended by saying they realised that some products could fail to function and if this was a rare case at my side I should feel free to write to the direct mail id of their head of customer relations, whose id this mail had been sent from.

Well, that's something positive, I thought to myself. I wondered where they'd got my mail id from. Then I remembered they had made me fill out a small form with my contact details on it after I had made the purchase. At that time I'd thought it was just another gimmick with the form being filed away into cold-storage, but apparently they had put it to good use.

This definitely is a positive Ketchup, a healthy sign of their intent. It's a good beginning, proactive. Now let's see if their follow up is as good, I wondered. Then I brought myself back to reality. Even if they do want to follow up on their promise what good would it do me? If I were in London it would be a different matter, but here I was on the other side of the ocean far away. No use.

Anyway, since they'd been good enough to write, let me at least give them a chance to do good. I did e-mail them from office at lunchtime. (Our organization permits all employees to use the net for personal mail). And then I forgot all about it and got absorbed in the daily routine of office work.

The very next day I got a response from them where they said, "We are really sorry about the problem you are facing. Please courier us the defective product at the following postal address and allow us to do the needful."

"Well, well," I said to myself, "That's a good sign. An immediate response. At least it shows that someone at their end is awake, alert, taking things seriously and doing their job."

The point is, it was not a mindless computer generated nameless response as happens so often. There was a name attached to the mail to which I could connect and write. A human contact point that had the decency to identify himself.

But couriering such a large parcel is expensive, and that too to the U.K. I promptly mailed them back thanking them for their immediate response.

I mentioned in my mail that couriering from India was an expensive proposition and would they really take any action once I couriered it or would I just be wasting my money.

Again immediately the next day I got a response to the effect, "Please leave it to us. We'll handle everything and solve the matter to your satisfaction. Could you just please take the trouble of couriering it to us. For us, customer satisfaction is the absolute priority. We won't let you down."

Once again the mail was sent by the same person who had also thoughtfully added his phone number if I needed to speak to him.

That certainly sounded reassuring.

I got the box to work the next day. When our office courier guy came, I asked him what the charges would be. Uh oh. Pretty steep.

I debated with myself. If I didn't take the initiative and courier it, anyway it would be 32 pounds down the drain. (That being the cost of the game). If I did trust them and courier it I could stand to lose more money with possibly no outcome.

"What the heck," I told myself. I always pride myself on giving everyone a second chance. These guys deserved it after their prompt response. On an impulse I couriered it, mentally writing the courier charges off as a loss.

Exactly a week later a large couriered parcel from Hamley's was awaiting me when I arrived home.

Farah said, "Umar was so excited that he wanted to unwrap it the moment it arrived, but I told him to wait for you."

I was as excited as Umar. I dropped my briefcase, got a cardboard cutter, and was about to cut it open when Farah said, "Chill, whatever is inside can wait. Have a shower, I'll make some soup and once we're all relaxed, we'll open it and see what's inside."

I fumbled with the cup of tea that Farah brought, had a shower in double quick time, and gulped down my soup.

Farah smiled. "I've got 2 kids in the house," she said.

I took the cardboard cutter and carefully opened the packing.

Under normal circumstances I would have ripped it open but it was so neatly and beautifully packed, someone had taken real care over it and I couldn't just savage it. I respected the effort the person had taken.

At last it was open. And can you believe the contents?

1.   A replaced game of the same model and type I had returned (which this time was in perfect working condition).

2.   A note mentioning that they had phoned my local courier by checking his telephone number on the courier docket, asked him the amount I had paid as courier charges, and they had written to me saying if I could mail them my bank account number they would reimburse me with the amount I had spent on couriering the defective piece to them.

3.   A gift voucher for 25 pounds valid for the next ten years for any product from their store when I visited London next.

4.   A personal, hand written letter from their chairman thanking me for couriering the product back, thus allowing him an opportunity to get feedback and serve me. In the letter he also personally apologised for the mental agony me and my son must have undergone by getting a product which didn't work in the first place.

"Man, I could have collapsed."

AMAAAAZING.

"And before somebody says that if they continue giving freebies like this they'll go out of business, **let me tell you they have been in business,** very successfully and profitably, for the last sixty years.

Any product can fail. Even rockets and missiles do. I realize that.

But what I expect when a product fails is that I be treated humanely, by the organisation putting itself in my shoes, not trying to defend itself with irritating excuses and hiding behind so called systems and procedures, but coming out forthrightly and doing what it takes to retain my loyalty and allowing me to give them a second chance.

These guys at Hamley's Toy Store **didn't need** to do all that they did to keep me satisfied. I was not a regular customer by any standard. I lived on the other side of the ocean.

The Mall in my city by contrast OUGHT to have taken more care. I was a regular customer myself and represented an organization giving them lakhs worth of business. But they were just not bothered. Inspite of my holding their Loyalty Card, no staff from the mall even recognised me as someone who had given more than twenty lakhs worth of business to them till I identified myself.

"You know Furqan, what you said right now holds true for any business and if we just keep probing we may find that eight out of ten service providers do a shabby job," chipped in Sunil. "But more than anything else I think the evening today has taught me how to behave with my own customers in my own business. I don't think I learned so much about customer service even during my MBA."

"You bet," added Harsh. "At the end of the day, each service provider is also a service receiver and vice versa."

"Guys, what about packing up. Its getting too late and got to go to work tomorrow morning," intervened Rahul.

"Ya. Lets get moving. And thanks Radhika for the wonderful hospitality," said Ushma.

"I am gonna remember this evening for long and I think henceforth all of us might just be observing Ketchups everywhere," added Harsh.

"Thanks once again Apurva," added Sunil. "And most importantly wish you all the best in your hunt for a caring caterer... Rare to find, I must add."

"Thanks," said Apurva. "You know, the insights I've gained this evening about identifying truly great service providers are really going to help me in taking my decision to appoint a caterer."

The single most important thing to remember about any enterprise is that there are no results inside its walls; the result of a successful business is a satisfied customer.

- Peter Drucker

Too often we underestimate the power of a touch, a smile, a kind word, a listening ear, an honest compliment, or the smallest acts of caring, all of which have the potential to turn a life around.

- Leo Buscaglia

We should give as we would receive; cheerfully, quickly and without hesitation.

\- Seneca

It is well to give when asked, but it is better to give unasked, through understanding.

\- Kahlil Gibran

10

The Decision

Apurva went to office on Monday and immediately immersed himself in work.

Around noon, Rajeev came to his cabin and asked, "So, how are you feeling now? Looks like you had a good weekend. Partied hard, huh? Or just a quiet time at home? Anyway you look much better than when I dropped you home on Saturday night."

"No man, just some old friends at home for dinner. Had a nice time," replied Apurva.

"Do you want to finalise that issue of the caterer today? I told you I'd solve your problem for you, didn't I? Mr Chavan from 'The Great Taste' has called me twice since morning already but I told him Monday mornings are busy for you and that I'd speak to you at lunchtime. I know he'll give us a good rate, he's pretty eager to break into the corporate world with a big client like us. Are you free after lunch? He's ready to come over and discuss the terms and conditions of the contract."

"I'm sorry," said Apurva, "But you'll have to give me a few days time to think it over and take a decision. Yes, I know the food he served was great and the ambience was terrific but I'm just not quite sure…"

Rajeev gave him a weird look and all he said was, "Well, it's your call. I just hope you know what you're doing."

It was now lunchtime. Apurva went up to the cafeteria. Saw the unhappy faces of people around. After mustering a lot of courage he casually asked one of them what the problem was today.

"The salad is already over and not even half of us have had our food as yet. This is getting to be a daily affair. If it's not one thing, it's another. And I've just started my diet. All I was going to have for lunch was soup and salad. And now the salad is all over before half of us have reached the canteen. What are you Admin. guys up to? Can't you control the caterer? After all, we're his Customers. These small things are irritating us big time. Normally after a hard morning's work people look forward to their lunch. Good food, rest, chatting with friends, having a smoke. But over here all we seem to do is go to the cafeteria and argue with the caterer over some issue or the other every day and screw up our mood. And the guy's just not bothered. It's affecting our work. These guys get such a huge volume of business from us and yet they take us for granted. And how much do they save with this stupid attitude of their's?"

Apurva could now hear other voices.

"There are about ten items on the menu daily. Soup, salad, bread, rice, dal, curd, a dry veg dish, a gravy veg dish, a non-veg dish and a sweet.

By getting a little less of one or two items a day and having them fall short, how great can the caterer's savings be? Definitely not enough to make a palace.

And on the other hand how much does the caterer stand to lose? **Everything.**

They think they're so smart, but if they open their eyes they'll realise that no caterer has lasted in this company for more than a year's time.

It's not that we staff just keep demanding a change of caterer just for the sake of it."

Apurva left the cafeteria in despair and started thinking as he threw himself on his couch.

Once a supplier (in this case the caterer), is well set and has understood the customer's requirements and is consistently doing a good job of fulfilling these requirements, the customer would like to stick with him rather than going through the headache of identifying a new supplier, drawing up a fresh contract, trying him out, getting him to understand our taste and way of working.

It's a two way process. Like in an Interview, just as much as the candidate needs the job for the salary it provides him, equally importantly the organisation is looking out for a good candidate to do the work.

The same holds true for a single retail customer as well. For example, when your regular newspaper delivery boy or milkman or washerman go on leave, you eagerly wait for them to return as soon as possible. These service providers know your routine

and your requirements. If you go to take a haircut, and your regular barber is not there, most people would go back and return later when he is there.

This proves that customers need the personalised service that a service provider gives, just as much as the service provider needs the business.

But in their search to make a quick extra buck, the service providers are killing the goose that lays the golden eggs.

Apurva thought that he wouldn't call these guys smart businessmen.

He'd call them stupid.

> *Profit in business comes from repeat customers, customers that boast about your service, and that bring friends with them.*
>
> - Edward Deming

He couldn't have put it better himself. It fitted in so perfectly with his ketchup memory and what all of them had been discussing over dinner yesterday.

It set him thinking. All this while he had been upset with the way the caterers had been short-changing the organisation, but at least he had always thought that in the process they'd been making an extra buck.

He had always secretly envied their business acumen.

Now he realised that more than cheating the customer, they'd been cheating themselves.

They were playing a game of lose-lose rather than the win-win they could so easily have made it.

Whether it's an individual retail customer or a large corporate key account.

Whether you're supplying airline seats, insurance, banking solutions, furniture or toilet paper.

The concept remains the same.

His thoughts were broken by a knock on the door and as luck would have had it, it was the caterer, smiling shamelessly and inviting him for lunch.

"I noticed you didn't have lunch, Sir."

"I kept aside some salad for you, Sir. I know you like salad," said the caterer.

Apurva couldn't take it any more and blasted him. "Yes, I like salad. And so do the other staff that came before me to the lunchroom but had to do without it. The only difference between me and them as far as you are concerned is that I pass your bill and they don't. Well, get this straight, you can take this salad back and only if you can ensure that all my staff get salad, can you get it back to my table as well."

The caterer left his cabin in a hurry.

Apurva called for a cup of tea. He then asked Rajeev to see him in his room.

"Rajeev, I just can't stand this current caterer guy and his attitude a day longer but at the same time I can't throw him out till I get a replacement. And to be honest let me tell you that the guy you recommended as a caterer is definitely not coming in. Judging by his past attitude, things would remain pretty much the same or may even get worse," spoke Apurva.

"Past attitude ? You mean you know him? Why didn't you tell me that evening while having dinner?", asked Rajeev.

"Let's not talk about it. I don't want to get depressed further," said Apurva packing his bag, "Need some time for myself... I know where to go."

Apurva left the office and drove down towards the locality where his previous office had been located, and parked and got out. He somehow loved walking through those bylanes......browsing through the books on the roadside stalls....

He could see some small restaurants, and hunger pangs dawned on him. He stopped at a wayside restaurant for a snack.

He sat down and looked around. He now took a professional interest in the food business. It was a small place, but neatly done up. Looked homely and clean. Smelt fresh. There were only seven tables, all of them, including the one at which he sat, were occupied.

As soon as he sat, water was immediately served and a menu card was politely handed over by a smiling waiter in a spic and span uniform. The menu was not vast but sufficient thought had gone into it and it provided a good range of fare.

A bottle of ketchup, (filled to the top) lay at the centre of every table, so that guests could help themselves to ketchup and not be at the mercy of the management.

> *Always serve too much hot fudge sauce on hot fudge sundaes. It makes people overjoyed and puts them in your debt.*
>
> — Judith Olney

There were a couple of nice scenic paintings on the walls. Apurva turned to look at the counter where the guy who handled the cash sat. A plump, jolly looking man who looked vaguely familiar. ("Was this my week to renew old acquaintances?", he wondered). The man looked at him and smiled.

The sandwich he had ordered arrived, looked very appetizing and was accompanied with a generous helping of salad on the plate.

He helped himself to some Ketchup from the bottle on the table. The Ketchup wasn't thinned down with water, but was rich and thick.

He felt in a better mood than he'd been in all day. Water in his glass was attentively refilled as soon as the glass was half empty. People at all the other tables were being attended to efficiently and courteously as well. He began to wish that this place were located closer to office, he would have come here for his lunch regularly. He finished the sandwich and the delicious salad. The salad hadn't just been dumped on the plate as an afterthought, but was clearly a planned exercise and very tasty by itself, with a touch of mayonnaise and mustard in it.

He called for the bill.

When his bill arrived, there was a small piece of sweetmeat provided with it.

He enquired from the waiter what the occasion was.

"No occasion, Sir. We always like our patrons to leave the restaurant with a sweet taste in their mouth. It's a small piece, but we want them to remember us well and we thrive on their good wishes and blessings."

> **Customers are investments, maximize your return.**
>
> - Peoplesoft Ad

"Where had I seen this sweet concept before? It looked familiar," thought Apurva to himself.

Apurva thanked the waiter and started to leave the place. On the way out, he paused to thank the gentleman at the counter for providing him with a great experience. Apurva thanked him; the man smiled back, their eyes met, and then RECOGNITION HIT.

"ANNA?", yelled Apurva.

The man at the counter replied, "Apu baba?"

He stepped out of the counter and they hugged each other.

Anna was the person who ran a small restaurant at Matunga about 10 years ago and Apurva had worked in an office nearby for a couple of years. That had been the only time during his working career that

Apurva hadn't needed to carry a tiffin, although Anna's was a small restaurant with no fancy menu. (There was only a FIXED menu which started getting served sharp at 12, piping hot lovely home cooked type food, a rice, dal, 2 vegetables, steaming hot chapaties, curd, and a fruit or a sweetmeat). All served brilliantly, yummy, and piping hot and unlimited. You could have as much as you liked, with Anna's only condition being that food on your plate should not be wasted. Apurva couldn't recall a single day in those 2 years when any item on the menu ever fell short. Those days, he used to eagerly await for lunchtime to arrive right from the time he reached work in the morning, wondering what tasty delicacy Anna had prepared that day. Looking back, he seriously thought the reason why he stuck to that job for 2 years was because he didn't want to work far off from Anna's restaurant.

All these thoughts raced through his mind as he joyfully hugged Anna.

"Anna... I am seeing you again after about 10 years and you are still the same. And of course, the policy of the guest always leaving with a sweet tooth I had first experienced from you. That's why it seemed so familiar," said a delighted Apurva.

Anna made him sit down at the table that he had just vacated and came over to join him. They exchanged stories about the last ten years. Apurva about his job, and Anna about his business. He told Apurva how he'd bought this place around five years ago. He mentioned that he'd also bought a kitchen nearby and had ventured into Industrial Catering. He had a few corporate clients, no big names among them yet, but then his philosophy had always been steady growth. First putting resources in place, not overstepping his capability, not biting off more than he could chew.

Apurva had a glint in his eyes. An idea grew in his mind. This was the solution he was looking for. He had found his caterer at last. The rest is just detail.

At first Anna was doubtful if he could handle that scale of operation but Apurva soon convinced him and he gained confidence. Apurva took him back to office with him so that he could see the cafeteria and setup. Anna got equally excited the moment he saw the setup and started asking questions about the tastes and preferences of the staff, and what was the staff cultural mix so that he could accordingly plan his menu.

This was something the other caterers so far had never bothered to ask. For them what mattered was that there would be ten items on the daily menu, lunch service would begin by 12.15 and wind up by 1.30, that's all that had been their focus. Oh yes, and the bill should be promptly paid.

But not so with Anna. He didn't get into the terms and conditions of the contract first, 50 % advance, the balance paid by the seventh of next month, etc.

Anna focused on **GIVING**, not **GETTING**.

Nobody's saying that terms and conditions are not important. They have to be clarified. But first let your customer realise that you are concerned about giving him the best that you can, before starting off on Rupees, Annas, and Paisa.

Again, like in an interview, of course salary is vital, but that's not what a good candidate will bring up first.

Apurva in turn went that evening to see Anna's kitchen where Anna prepared his corporate meals, and Anna encouraged Apurva to chat with his staff.

Apurva was surprised to see that most of the staff Anna had in his kitchen were the same people he had with him 10 years ago. That definitely told a tale by itself.

Apurva came to work the next day elated and called for Rajeev.

"Guess what ? I've finally decided on the caterer," said a relieved Apurva.

"That's great news," said Rajeev. "So at last you've made up your mind. Should I ring up Mr. Chavan of 'The Great Taste' and tell him to come over or do you want to go there this evening, tell him you've decided, and sample his food again?"

"It's not him, Rajeev. It's someone else."

Rajeev got a shock of his life when Apurva told him about Anna.

"Are you crazy? You must be out of your mind," he said. "How can you compare the two? It's like comparing chalk and cheese. Look at the experience in Corporate Catering that Mr. Chavan has. Look at the resources at his command."

Apurva told him, "Many a miser has died with kilos of gold under his bed. A caterer may have all the ketchup in the world but if he doesn't put it on the table when required, what use is it? People don't go around drinking ketchup, do they? Nor do people like to waste. Some people like a little more mayonnaise or ketchup with their meal or more sugar in their tea than others. So? Should the service provider dictate their taste to them? Sorry. No way."

> **Resources by themselves are of no value without the right attitude and the heart to use them.**
>
> - Cyrus M. Gonda & Kalim Khan

Anna started serving his food within fifteen days. At first people were skeptical.

And again there were voices.

"Another new caterer? That means we'll get good meals at least for a week or two."

That was one of the typical, sarcastic comments passed by the staff the moment they heard of the new caterer. But over a period of time, their skepticism changed to respect. Rather than deteriorate in quality, over a period of time, the staff's dining experience actually improved.

This was because Anna visited the office premises regularly, and his hand-picked supervisors went out of their way to take feedback from the staff about their favourite dishes, new things they'd like to see introduced in the menu, etc. And the staff, once they realized that their feedback was being taken seriously and being given the importance it deserved by implementation, eagerly awaited meal times and the opportunity to interact with the service providers. Very rarely a particular dish did fall short, but Anna compensated in his unique way by providing an extra special menu the next day. Every religious festival got the importance it deserved on the meal table, with Anna providing special festival fare.

He ensured that his staff were courteous and always wore clean uniforms. It was not in his contract to keep the cafeteria area clean, yet he insisted on his boys doing the cleaning anyway after the regular cleaning was done by the office staff.

"A second cleaning never hurts," Anna said. "Besides it's a place where people eat their meals. It needs to be as hygienic as possible." Another WOW from Anna.

The salt and pepper shakers were always cleaned and filled. Never empty.

If there was a Chinese dish on the menu on a particular day, Anna made sure that all the Chinese sauces were provided in bottles on every table.

He also added a nice touch of a small flower vase on every table and a fresh rose in each one everyday.

He bought a deodorant spray and ensured the dining room smelt fresh as a daisy at all times.

He decided the menu for the day a week in advance and put up the menu for the entire next week on the dining room notice board so that if people didn't prefer the dishes he was serving on a particular day, they could plan in advance and get their tiffins from home on that day or decide to eat out and plan their meal rather than coming up to the dining room, seeing that the dish was something which was not to their taste, by which time it would be too late to go down for a meal outside.

Previous caterers had not permitted employee's guests to dine, saying it disturbed their calculation for the quantity of food to be served for the staff, and then they gave that as a reason for food falling short. Anna welcomed guests. Of course the employees paid for their guests, but the point is that he didn't say that it disturbed his food count. As he put it, on any given day there couldn't be more than twenty guests and that's a number he could easily take care of. It's all a matter of Mindset and Attitude once again.

Although the official time for lunch ended at 1.45 p.m., Anna realized that it was a Corporate environment, staff could be busy, get late, come from an outside sales call, and definitely be in the mood for a nice hot meal. The previous caterers had started removing the dishes at 1.45 sharp and if any of the staff walked in then, rather than welcoming them, they were literally humiliated by the catering staff for walking in late and messing up their schedule. But not Anna. He didn't behave like a Prison Guard or treat the place like a Military Camp. In such cases, he didn't watch the clock, but made staff feel welcome and kept the meal hot for them even 30 minutes after the scheduled close of lunch time.

And speaking of clocks, the cafeteria had a wall clock in the dining room. It was a normal battery operated clock and when the battery got over, the previous caterers had never bothered to even inform the Administration staff about the same in case they hadn't noticed.

But in Anna's case it was different.

A particular afternoon, one of the office Admin. staff saw the clock had stopped and he instructed the peon to replace the battery the next morning. But when the peon went the next morning, the battery had already been replaced. He asked Anna's staff about it and they mentioned that they'd got a battery from outside and changed it themselves. **They said that Anna had told them to take care of this place as if it were their own home and any immediate expenses they needed to make, he gave them an advance amount for the same.**

> *There are no traffic jams along the extra mile.*
> > - Roger Staubach

This was just a small sample of the numerous things that Anna and his staff did to change the previously ordinary dining room into a haven of good food, rest and relaxation.

> *Be faithful in small things, because it is in them that your strengh lies.*
> > - Mother Teresa

And Anna's staff were not Hotel Management College graduates, nor were they MBA's and neither was Anna an MBA himself.

It just proves that qualifications are good, experience is great, but Attitude is vital and best of all.

"So Rajeev, how is the cafeteria doing now?", asked Apurva one day, with a victorious smile on his face.

"This man Anna has turned around the place. The staff just seems to love him. I wouldn't be surprised if he is the singular most important cause of our staff retention rate improving," admitted Rajeev.

"I can't tell you how happy everyone is at office now and especially at meal times. It has enhanced the feel good factor and consequently the overall productivity. Even the visitors who come to our office have noticed the positive difference in the way our staff attends to them ever since Anna has started catering," said Apurva.

"Thank God I didn't go with that flashy caterer and restaurant owner that you had suggested. He would, I'm sure have added to our misery after the first two weeks of catering," continued Apurva.

"And all because of his stinginess with a bottle of ketchup 15 years ago," smiled Rajeev.

"You bet... And one thing I've learned out of all this is how to identify and select the best service provider out of all the options you have available," added Apurva.

"What's that?", asked Rajeev.

> *"Stick with the service provider with the biggest heart and you won't go wrong."*
>
> *- Cyrus M. Gonda & Kalim Khan*

11

The Message

After a few months of Anna doing the catering, one fine day Rajeev came in to Apurva's cabin for a cup of tea. While chatting in general, the topic of caterers came up. Rajeev was honest enough to admit that Anna was doing a fantastic job.

"But how did you initially have such confidence that he would do so well? You hadn't met him for years," he said.

"Look over here," Apurva said with a smile.

He made a small black dot on a white blank foolscap paper and asked him what he saw there.

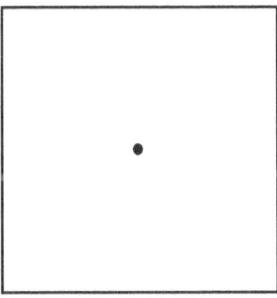

Rajeev confidently answered, "A black dot! of course."

Apurva replied triumphantly, "That's precisely the point. The black dot doesn't even cover 1 % of the surface area on the paper. 99 % of what you see is a clean, white sheet. Yet you ignored the sheet and focused on the tiny black dot."

Rajeev replied, "But the white sheet is so obvious. That's why I focused on the black dot."

"Yes. That's exactly my point. The basic requisites in any product or service are obvious. Any car will have an engine, steering, windscreen, four wheels, and the rest. It's the detail and the finish, the attitude of going out of the way, **that 1% extra** that distinguishes and sets apart one organisation's products, services and finally it's reputation from the others in the same industry.

It's that 0.01 second difference which wins a gold medal at the Olympic Games. Take a 100 meter sprint, the gold medal may be won by someone with a timing of 9.95 seconds and the silver may go to someone with a time of 9.96. That's the way it goes. But who bothers about the silver medallist? No one. But the gold medallist wins immortal fame. Difference between the two? 0.01%.

The Winner takes it all.

Yes, Rajeev, you are absolutely right. The white sheet is more than 99 % of what you saw, yet you ignored it, because that's obvious. That's given. It's expected. Nobody focuses on it. Neither did you. The white sheet, which is the basic 99 %, if present, doesn't lure or attract people.

It's that 1 % extra which you provide, that's remembered and talked about.

> *You cannot improve one thing by 1000 % but*
> *you can improve 1000 little things by 1%.*
>
> - Jan Carlzon, CEO, Scandinavian Airways

"The personal touch, the attitude of caring, the items that don't reflect in the final bill, yet are more vital than the tangibles that do reflect in the bill. They matter the most."

> *God is in the details, the Devil is in the details you*
> *overlook. Focus on the details; win the love of your*
> *customers. Omit, ignore, overlook details, and win*
> *the love of your competition. Whose love would you*
> *rather win?*
>
> - Cyrus M. Gonda & Kalim Khan

"It's the same reason that enlightened recruiters today say, 'We hire for attitude and we train for skill.'

I have now decided that when I appoint any supplier or even select a service provider in my personal life, first I will check if he has a generous attitude, and even in my absence, when I'm not around, his heart and hand will then be just as big and generous," emphasised Apurva.

Apurva then told Rajeev about the conversations he had with his friends during that evening dinner six months ago.

About the healthy Attitude of the staff at the Govinda Restaurant in Isckon, Paris Bakery, and the two old guys running their bakery in Nashik, the Toyshop in U.K., (Hamley's), and all the other service greats that he and his friends had discussed about in their evening meet at his place.

What differentiated them from their competitors? What made their customers so loyal to them and return to them, coming back again and again and again even if these places were not as conveniently located as their competitors were?

The eye for detail, the nurturing caring, and the empathy that made the customer feel that it was a loving family member looking after them and caring for them.

About how when we go to a particular service provider to satisfy our needs, we yearn to be attended to caringly. We are willing to pay a premium to a provider who will do that, yet in most cases we are disappointed and our expectations come crashing down. And we all know what happens then. It's just a monotonous, fragile, lethargic transaction, and the customer is desperate to find alternatives, and in today's competitive environment, that's not too difficult, or is it?

Such simple lessons but so rarely are they applied."

> *People expect good service, but few are willing to give it.*
> - Robert Gately, President, Gately Consulting

"It's like every student knows that in order to get a good score at the end of the year, the logical steps to take are; attend all the lectures, keep all the notes, study regularly, pay attention and ask questions. There's no complicated formula associated. And students who follow these simple steps succeed. Yet how many students follow these simple steps? In the same way all organisations know that these are the basic recipes for success. But in the day to day affairs of business these important basics somehow get swept aside.

The service provider who doesn't focus on these details may be attractive and glamorous, but that's a surface picture. Below the surface the attitude sucks. I wouldn't trust him with my back turned and I obviously can't be around all the time," continued Apurva. "Like you remember the previous caterer didn't get sufficient salad for the staff but kept aside a good portion for me as I'm the one who signs the bill. That's not the type of supplier I'm looking out for.

It's like an employee who only works hard when the boss is around, and who wants a guy like that."

> *The greatest discovery of my generation is that human beings can alter the quality of their lives by altering their attitude.*
>
> - William James, Psychologist

"I would go a step further and say that human beings can not only alter the quality of their own lives, but also the lives of **OTHERS** around them as well by altering their own attitude," continued Apurva.

Rajeev said, "But don't you feel you're carrying it too far? After all, the incident with the ketchup you're talking about happened about 15 years ago."

Apurva then reminded him about the Aesop's fable of the leopard unable to change his spots, or the dog's tail remaining crooked. These are stories which have been handed down through generations and are still as relevant today.

In fact most corporate trainers use these ancient stories from Aesop, Panchatantra, Mythology, to pass on important corporate messages today. There is a wealth of truth in these timeless fables.

You must have definitely heard of that English proverb, "Give a dog a bad name and hang him." It means once your reputation is spoilt due to even one bad incident, it becomes very difficult to regain it. Everybody then remembers and associates you with that one negative incident. And in today's competitive environment this has become even more relevant.

Once you disappoint someone, it becomes very difficult to trust that person again. Especially when there are so many competitors eagerly awaiting for half a chance.

After all, the customer is spending his hard earned money. Why should he go to a service provider who has already disappointed him in the past, however long back it may have been? There are many other service providers waiting for a chance to serve him better.

> *Customers don't care how big you are. They don't care about organizational charts or how many divisions you have. They want the person in front of them to be able to solve their problem.*
>
> - Vernn R. Loucks Jr., Chairman & CEO, Baxter International Inc.

It's not a question of the chef's competency. That was never in doubt. There are many people who can cook a tasty meal.

It's attitude that counts. Attitude defines altitude.

> *Ability is what you're capable of doing.*
> *Motivation determines what you do.*
> *Attitude determines how well you do it.*
>   - Lou Holtz

"Entry in business comes through the meal. But sustenance comes through the ketchup."

That's why companies with excellent reputations for service spend maximum time on identifying good people in the selection and interviewing process. Once that's there, the rest falls in place. The system then takes over.

Apurva added, "Please understand, I've not taken this decision to not appoint Mr. Chavan out of vindictiveness or revenge. That's not my style. I would never let personal likes and dislikes impact my professional decisions. **The reason I rejected the caterer you recommended was that his only aim was short term profit.** Though I agree he has access to better resources.

Try to understand that no customer wants to change service providers for the sake of changing. The very fact that you want to change indicates your dissatisfaction."

There is a urban myth that customer service is unique to specific sectors. Utter balderdash. The skills needed are the same, whether you work in a hotel, an exhaust fitters, the town hall, or a hair saloon.

- Robert Crawford, Director, ICS

"We keep going to a restaurant where they know our tastes and understand our needs. I go regularly to a restaurant where they understand my need for ketchup and without my asking they put it on the table for me without any fuss, whatever be the dish I have ordered. That's how I would choose."

> *People only change service providers when the pain of tolerance is more than the pain of change.*
>
> - Cyrus M. Gonda & Kalim Khan

"Basic psychology says that human beings take any action for only one of two reasons. First, to move towards pleasure, and second, to move away from pain. The same applies to the actions that customers take."

"Changing service providers also has a cost attached to it. Why do you as a service provider want to increase the cost of tolerance of your poor service to your customers so that it outweighs the cost of change for them?

I have developed a formula to identify the stage at which a customer will decide to change his service provider.

It happens *when P is greater than C.*

Where P stands for The Pain caused due to continuing with the current service provider. And C being the Cost of Change.

Every time you have an interaction with another individual, you change your opinion about him one way or the other. Based on that last interaction you had, your opinion is slightly modified one way or another. If someone does an unexpected good gesture, his value in your mind goes up and vice versa. One very bad incident can totally destroy a long standing relation forever.

But you require more than resources to do a good job of delighting the customer.

A diamond, which is a great resource, lying in the mine has no value till it is extracted and cut and polished.

A service provider's resources will be of no value if his intention of utilising those resources to the fullest extent to satisfy the customers is simply not there.

With all the resources in the world, if the attitude is not correctly tuned, it is as good as having no resources at all.

Broke is not a state of pocket, it is a state of mind."

> *Good customer service costs less than bad customer service.*
> - Sally Gronow, Welsh Water Corporation

"Mr. Chavan will drown in his ketchup, but not provide it for his customer's taste buds. Like some fruit vendors who will let their fruits rot, but not sell them at a reasonable price.

That man will let the ketchup pass the expiry date and then throw it in the dustbin, but not give it to a customer who would relish it and remember the meal he had with gratitude.

And the customer is not a fool. These are the apparently little things which for him are very big things. You have to look at it from the customer's perspective. These are the things he observes, notes in his mind, talks to others about, and bases his future decisions on.

Every separate incident that a customer faces is not dependent on past incidents but is a stand alone incident.

One negative incident can leave such a bad taste in the mouth that the person may never come back again.

It is human tendency to focus on negative experiences.

We can't change or control that. What we can control is our attitude as service providers, to ensure that every interaction is a positive one, and minimise or eliminate the negative.

Don't dilute the ketchup either by adding water. In other words don't compromise on quality of raw material or product or service thinking that people won't notice.

They will. So often in a food joint, don't we say yuck, this is cheap pumpkin ketchup, or, they've added water to the ketchup and diluted it.

All customers notice though all of them may not openly complain. But they will gradually move away to other service providers."

> *It's very easy to compromise quality a little at a time and it may be very tempting as a supplier to do so as well. But that's the road to business failure. It starts with a little at a time. Then the 'little' becomes a tidal wave.*
>
> — Cyrus M. Gonda & Kalim Khan

"And as the quality of your products and services drop, your customer's confidence and trust in you will drop, and so will your sales, and ultimately your profits.

Then such companies resort to window dressing and glamorous advertisements."

Don't polish the leaves, first nurture the roots.
-Cyrus M. Gonda & Kalim Khan

"Rather than follow that route to failure, create an environment by doing the little things that cannot be duplicated by your competitors. Because these little things are not based on technology, which is neutral and can be bought by all; but are based on employees who can be attracted by a superior work culture and environment. Otherwise there is no differentiation, as everyone is selling almost a similar product almost at the same price.

The more technology we use, the more our social skills weaken, like a muscle that is rarely used and becomes weak. More time ought to be spent on learning and acquiring soft skills rather than hard skills. The problem is, we take soft skills for granted, but that's our greatest error.

Take care with details. Act as if you are the user and consumer and not the seller and service provider. For example when making a cocktail, which is a mixture of many drinks, you take all the ingredients in a shaker and shake it with ice. Then you pour it out and serve it. For the next cocktail, you use the same shaker and should ideally change the ice because if you use the old ice some of the ingredients of the previous cocktail are still stuck to it and their taste will be added here. Because it is time consuming and takes effort and more ice, normally people avoid changing the ice as it does not make THAT BIG A DIFFERENCE.

But it still makes a difference which can be made out especially if you are used to perfection. But if you are making a cocktail for yourself you would like perfection and would not mind the extra effort of changing the ice."

> *Don't treat a customer like a king. The king may not be related to you. Hence there may be no emotions involved from your side. Treat the customer like your day old child. Then only will you do your absolute best for him. Then you will succeed in delighting him.*
>
> — Cyrus M. Gonda & Kalim Khan

"Similarly while preparing a sweet cocktail, ideally you frost the glass which means you dip the tip of the glass in sugar syrup, make it sweet and sticky and then dip it in powdered sugar. That's a very nice touch, an extra which you can give which will really go the extra mile in pleasing the customer, but not everyone does it. You can also still go a step further and have chilled the glass itself beforehand in a freezer. So you see, there is so much to learn about going extra miles even in a simple thing like making a cocktail.

Some of the biggest brands are failing today for lack of service. Its all about service and relationship. No customer gives a second chance in today's competitive environment.

The looser the knot tying you and the customer together, the more easily it comes apart. If your magnet is weak and the competitor's magnet is stronger, your customer (the piece of iron you want to attract), will go to the stronger magnet."

> *Remember that iron (the customer), is neutral.*
> *It's the stronger magnet (service provider),*
> *which will succeed in attracting it.*
> - Cyrus M. Gonda & Kalim Khan

"Let me tell you what I've learnt from corporate life over the years. It's my humble learning and I don't mind sharing it with you. I want you to do well in life. In fact I want all businesses to do well. India is a global force to be reckoned with. Why lose out in the global race just due to lack of a healthy attitude?

If you open your own business, whichever field it may be, keep the following points in mind. They are universally applicable.

1. Select the "Right" People.

    "People" People.

    "Friendly" People.

    "Helpful" People.

    "Smiley" People.

2. Give them all the training you feel is necessary, and a little more, so that they can serve your customers to the best of their ability.

3. Empower and authorise them to take On the Spot decisions **so that customers get their issues resolved on the spot and issues are closed rather than escalated.** And to ensure that they take the correct decisions on the spot, the training they've been provided will enable them to do so.

4.   Give your employees a singular clear objective, that is, ***Satisfy and Delight the Customer.***

5.   Motivate your staff; preferably motivate each one individually as per their needs, so they are retained for as long a time as possible, so that they can know the customers well and your customers know them well. It's ridiculous that some organisations transfer staff because they don't want staff to get comfortable in one place. That's such a wrong philosophy. You're starting off with the basic premise of mistrusting your own people.

6.   Don't be short staffed at any point of time. It's not humanly possible for your staff to have an eye for detail and focus on providing excellent service when they don't even have enough time to perform their core activity and basic job.

Most of the things that customers yearn for don't require much expenditure. What they require is thoughtful effort and foresight.

Like selecting a gift for a friend, it's the thought that counts as much as the gift. No one says all this is easy, but the rewards are well worth it.

And all this is difficult for your competitors to duplicate.

And this becomes your U.S.P. (Unique Selling Point).

We talk so much about branding, but it is a fact that in any service industry, branding is all about the level of customer service provided.

And understand this one vital lesson. All it takes to turn existing low standards of service in any industry upside down is for one significant player in each industry to enhance the service level, and this doesn't require any high level of technology. All other players will have to follow unwillingly by default or else close shop. Wouldn't your organization like to be that ONE initiator? Think of all the benefits that go with it. First mover advantage, a permanent positive imprint on customers' mind, strong reputation that's hard to beat.

Logically think. All individuals want the best returns on investment. So do companies, so do customers. Makes sense. The customer is investing Time, Trust , Effort and Opportunity Cost of not going to another service provider. Naturally he'll stay or gravitate towards one who gives him maximum returns in terms of attention, care, empathy and eye for detail.

Little things matter the most.

> *A trifle consoles us, because a trifle upsets us.*
> - Blasé Pascal

Mistakes can happen. That we accept. (Although too many mistakes point to sheer negligence and apathy).

But how mistakes are **handled** is vitally important.

That impacts the judgement and opinion that the customer develops about the organisation for all future transactions.

Ask yourself honestly, "What type of Ketchup do my customers see my organisation as, Positive, Average or Negative?"

In fact KETCHUP could be a perfect analogy for good and for bad services that organisations provide. The **Goodness** would encompass:

K   Kindness

E   Empathy

T   Trustworthiness

C   Care

H   Honesty

U   Uniqueness

P   Putting It All Together

OR CONVERSELY, the Negative could stand for :

K   Kill Relationships

E   Estrange Yourself from Customer's Requirements

T   Taking the Customer for Granted

C   Carelessness

H   Haggling Over Trifles

U   Underhand Dealings

P   Pride

"You might as well take some lectures on management, Apurva," remarked Rajeev.

"It is not about lectures or big talks. I myself am a service provider to my own staff and I realise the importance of a delighted customer. And that can only consistently happen when I as a service provider instil in myself an Attitude of Service.

You might have heard of that concept of assigning a number to an alphabet sequentially. For example A = 1, B = 2... so on till Z = 26. In this way:

M-O-N-E-Y totals 72 (M = 13, O = 15, N = 14, E = 5, Y = 25)

Similarly, K N O W L E D G E totals 96

L U C K is only 47

L E A D E R S H I P at 97 falls short of 100 by 3

H A R D   W O R K reaches 98

It is A T T I T U D E which totals 100.

It is a very good concept and quite commonly known, but I would say it is incomplete. In today's age, 100 is simply not enough. And Attitude by itself is not a recipe for success.

I have devised my own formula.

Today, I feel that **SERVICE ATTITUDES** is the mantra for success. **And guess what**?

SERVICE ATTITUDES totals 200."

"I understand SERVICE, but why the **plural** in ATTITUDES?", asked Rajeev.

"ATTITUDES in Plural, simply because it has to exist in EVERYONE, for EVERYBODY and inevitably EVERYWHERE. No weak links permissible. And when you reach 200%, you are a cut above the competitors."

"Great. Excellent," said Rajeev.

"I would prefer to call this a necessity today. Excellence is the bare minimum a service provider needs to provide," said Apurva.

"You know, I have to rush back home early. Got another party with the same group. We all thought that the dinner we had was a real eye opener and a value add. Trust me since that evening we've all been on the lookout for KETCHUPS," continued Apurva, "And we meet regularly to share our KETCHUPS with each other."

"Can I invite myself?", smiled Rajeev.

"Sure," said Apurva. "Just carry your KETCHUP along and take my word, soon every person in the whole world is going to be discussing their own KETCHUP."

Dessert

The Icing on the Cake

The service related incidents we've covered through the length of this book, some literally horrifying, nevertheless accurate; others almost spiritually uplifting, all have a common thread linking them with one another. They all pertain to what are traditionally classified as "Service Industries."

But what we now wish to relate is an incident which we were fortunate to personally witness, just as this book was about to go into print.

This incident so impressed us, that we felt we simply had to conclude this book with this Mount Everest sized Ketchup. What is unique about what you will now read is the fact that the episode pertains to what has been dubbed the FMCG Sector, where there is little that an individual retail customer could normally expect in terms of customer service from the manufacturer's end.

The FMCG Industry deals with the manufacturing and marketing of products of daily use, such as soaps, biscuits, toothpastes, etc. and to be frank we never ever thought that the concept of Customer Service was really applicable in all it's elements to this industry, especially since rarely is there any interaction between the FMCG Company and the Retail Customer.

Contrary to this generally held belief, what we experienced and are keen to share with as many people as possible is something relating to this FMCG Industry, something which is so positively outstanding, it took our breath away.

HERE GOES.

The mother of one of us authors recently purchased a family pack plastic tub of Kwality Walls Ice Cream which has recently been introduced in new attractive flavours.

The tub was left unopened in our freezer, until one day some unexpected guests dropped in.

The weather being sweltering hot, all the guests readily agreed to have some ice-cream when it was offered.

She went to the kitchen and spent nearly fifteen minutes trying to open the plastic tub of ice cream by trying to follow the vague instructions depicted on the tub. The cover of the tub was resistant to all efforts to open, and ultimately the guests had to settle for soft drinks, creating quite an embarassing situation for the hostess.

She wrote off a letter to the Company Address mentioned on the tub that very same day, expressing disgust with the vague instructions and diagram which led to this situation.

A pleasant surprise in the form of a prompt response to the letter arrived from the company.

Following is the letter we received.

Copy of the Letter

Hope this letter finds you in the best of health and cheers.

We are very grateful for your time and for your feedback. We strive very hard to ensure that every occasion our consumers eat ice cream is a special memorable moment and leaves them smiling. Consumer experiences like yours form the foundation for our efforts to improve our products and our consumer's experience.

Every year we introduce innovative products in the market place in line with consumer expectations. This summer saw us launching the Selection range in tub format. As you are aware there are indeed four flavours; Fruit 'n' Nut, Mocha Brownie Fudge, Cookies 'n' Cream and Caramel Crunch.

The tub design was evolved after extensive consumer research and development on the flavours & mixes to deliver the desired product quality at the point of consumption. The tub has been equipped with a tamper-proof seal to maintain the product quality, texture and goodness as when packed. It also makes it convenient to store the product over a longer duration in the home-freezer letting our consumers enjoy the same over a period of time.

It is unfortunate that a part of your experience with the tub was not as desired. We have in fact listened to suggestions such as yours to include a visual mnemonic on the sticker to help our consumers "break-the-seal" before they attempt to lift the lid from the groove.

Meanwhile I would be very grateful if you could grant me 10 Minutes of your time; to come over to your house to deliver a sample with our compliments and also demonstrate to you how the seal works. Please do call me at (telephone number), and tell me of a time that is convenient to you.

We take this very seriously and cannot appreciate it enough. I have forwarded this to the entire team and they are working on ideas that will ensure that; henceforth you and none of our consumers face a similar predicament.

I await your call.

Sincerely yours,

Deepak Sub

Brand Executive

Kwality Walls

There are some brilliant points to be picked up from this incident by any individual or organisation genuinely interested in raising the bar of service in their organisation.

First, the letter itself. It is not a standard format letter sent out routinely by a clerk in the despatch department.

Great thought has gone into the letter and it is highly customised, polite, descriptive, and customer focused.

Next, when we called the Executive who had sent this letter, he immediately recognised the incident we were referring to when we mentioned our name.

He wished a cheerful Good Morning and said, "Please tell me when you'd like me to come over with a sample to make up for the inconvenience, and also to demonstrate the correct method of opening the tub, which is really rather simple, though I agree it is not correctly described on the tub itself."

We said there was no need to do that and we had merely written to give our feedback, but he insisted on coming and even asked which flavour we would prefer.

We mentioned a time and day when it would be convenient to us and he turned up exactly at that time. Unlike the delivery of expensive washing machines and refrigerators which is often delayed beyond all belief, Deepak Sub took time out and turned up exactly when we requested and he promised.

This itself was another positive ketchup.

When he arrived, he got with him not one, but two tubs, one being the flavour we had requested and another good flavour which he had selected for us.

He also presented us with a carry case made of a special material we could use in future for carrying the tub outside if required. Throughout the letter he sent us or the conversation he had with us, HE GAVE NO EXCUSES.

Not in the least did we get the feeling, either through word or tone, that he considered us dumb idiots for not being able to open a tub of ice-cream.

He carefully and gently demonstrated how the tub was to be opened so that in future we would not have a problem. He left after thanking us for giving him an opportunity to rectify the lacunae on behalf of his organisation.

All this amply proves that providing Excellent Customer Service is not the responsibility or prerogative of Service Industries alone. Any organisation in any industry can differentiate itself positively through excellent service.

In fact, if you ponder, a soap is a soap is a soap, or a toothpaste is a toothpaste is a toothpaste, at least for the layman who doesn't understand the technical intricacies and chemical composition of these products. What will separate one organisation from another in even a manufacturing industry will increasingly be the attention to customer needs and quality of positive interaction that the organisation undertakes.

We are NOT the Advertising Department of Hindustan Unilever or Kwality Walls, but as we have expressed throughout this book, excellence and effort MUST be rewarded.

After all, this is what Word of Mouth Publicity is all about.

The Organisation we just referred to, being a Rs. 10,000 crore plus FMCG giant need not have bothered about us, who are comparatively ants. But they did. And they did so splendidly, proving that the best organisations in any industry, especially in this era of cut-throat competition and dropping margins, realise that only GOOD SERVICE IS GOOD BUSINESS.

We have now personally become raving fans of HUL, whereas previously we really didn't differentiate one FMCG Company from another. Now we have started to look out for the name of the PARENT COMPANY on an FMCG Product before we see the BRAND NAME OF THE SOAP OR TOOTHPASTE, not because we feel their products are superior to their competitors (we are not the experts in that), but we do realise that even if we are not satisfied with the product for some reason, the management of the company is firmly there behind each Individual Retail Customer, who INDIVIDUALLY MAY BE AN ANT, BUT COLLECTIVELY FORMS THE COMPANY'S ENTIRE CUSTOMER BASE. The customer base of even a giant organisation is like a swarm of locusts or grass hoppers, who are INDIVIDUALLY SO INSIGNIFICANT, BUT COLLECTIVELY SWARMS OF THESE LOCUSTS HAVE WIPED OUT THE CROPS OF ENTIRE CONTINENTS WITHIN A MATTER OF DAYS.

This is the point that even the largest Organisation in the world needs to remember.

A LAYMAN CUSTOMER MAY NOT BE AN EXPERT IN PRODUCT KNOWLEDGE OR MANUFACTURING, BUT HE IS DEFINITELY AN EXPERT IN EVALUATING THE KIND OF SERVICE HE RECEIVES. THERE IS NO DOUBT THAT HE IS THE BEST PERSON TO JUDGE THAT.

We now have full faith that we can count on exceptional care, professional communication, promptness in response and a highly personalised touch should we wish for some reason to communicate with HUL.

IN SHORT, WE KNOW THAT THE ELEPHANT WILL POSITIVELY RESPOND TO THE ANT.

Another point that emerges is that if they take such effort and care over a single retail customer, who realistically forms only a totally insignificant micro percentage of their turnover, imagine the efforts they must be taking to satisfy their large corporate accounts.

This is totally the opposite approach to that displayed for example by soft drink firms. When a customer complains to them about overcharging by a dealer for selling the drink chilled, in most cases we have heard that the Soft Drink Giants care two hoots for the individual customer. The only response he gets in most cases to such a complaint is silence.

Thus, though this book talks of the story of a person in search of a good corporate supplier (an office caterer), the message of this book is equally applicable for suppliers dealing with individual retail customers as well. In fact, the reason that Apurva, the protagonist of this book, decided not to go ahead with a particular caterer for his office was because he had a negative experience as an individual retail customer with this same supplier many years ago.

You never know as a service provider which of your customers have a vast circle of influence which could affect your business postively or negatively, now or in the future, depending on how you treat them every single time they interact with you.

We could go on with more examples but we feel that the icing on the cake should not be too thin, or too thick, but just right for our customers, our readers, whether they be Service Receivers or Service Providers, to get the message.

Because we realise that even a book has CUSTOMERS, YOU, OUR DEAR READERS who can help us spread the good word about how to bring Indian Industry to its rightful prime position in the Global Corporate Arena by delighting all customers through outstanding service.

All the very best in your efforts to reach the peak of Service Excellence.

Profile

KALIM KHAN

You may find many who like to follow the beaten path. But you will find only a few who dare to think beyond, and leave a trail behind. Kalim Khan is one of them. A quantitative expert, a soft skill genius, a provocative speaker, a management guru, a thought leader, a corporate advisor - these are just a few roles Kalim Khan plays in his daily life.

Coming from an academically rich background, Kalim is an MBA in Marketing, and a Production Engineer, both attained from the University of Mumbai.

He conducts regular workshops and training programmes in areas such as Application of Quantitative Techniques in Management, Problem Solving and Decision Making, Productivity Improvement, 6 Sigma, Sales Training and others for leading corporate houses including Philips, Tata Motors, Godrej, Mahindra & Mahindra, Colgate Palmolive, Wockhardt, Crompton Greaves, etc. Kalim's proven expertise in System and 5S Audits and Kaizen has earned him the privilege of implementing several projects in reputed organizations. Additionally, he also has industry experience at executive level in manufacturing as well as marketing in reputed organizations.

Currently, Kalim is serving as the Director of the prestigious Rizvi Institute of Management Studies and Research at Bandra. Leveraging on his outstanding contributions, this Institution has steadily charted its way up the ladder and is currently amongst the top ranked Management Institutes in Mumbai. He is also a Member of the Business Advisory Committee of Central Depository Services (India) Limited.

Profile

CYRUS M. GONDA

Cyrus is a rank holder MBA from University of Mumbai as well as a rank holder in Hotel Management. He is also a life member of MENSA, the International Society of Individuals with genius level IQ. He has work experience in Operational as well as Administrative areas in Fortune 500 organisations in the Service as well as Manufacturing Sectors both in India and overseas. For the last ten years he has been involved with Management Education, Corporate Training and Consultancy. He has trained over 50,000 individuals in B-Schools and Corporates, including senior Indian Army and Navy Officers.

He is currently H.O.D. – General Management with Rizvi Institute of Management Studies and Research, and the Vice Principal (All India), of the National Institute of Event Management. He is a visiting faculty in areas of Marketing and Service Sector Management in leading Management Institutes across Mumbai. His areas of interest include a passion for Improvement in Customer Service and Process and Systems Improvement.

He undertakes consultancy assignments in the areas of Customer Experience Enhancement, World Class Selling Techniques and Presentation Skills. He has a fantastic eye for detail and a keen and analytical mind. He draws upon his own life experiences to provide deliverables that enhance the bottom line in the training programmes that he conducts for organisations such as Godrej, VSNL, Mahindra & Mahindra, Tata Westside, Wockhardt, Della Tecnica and Oriental Bank of Commerce.

He is also a regular member for selection panels and discussions conducted by Corporate houses and B-Schools on various aspects of Management.

Profile

BRAINS TRUST

Both Kalim and Cyrus are the Joint Managing Directors of Brains Trust India, a Management Consultancy providing quantifiable deliverables which strengthen the bottom line in the areas of Customer Experience Management, Systems and Process Mapping, Creative Content Development, Six Sigma, Quality Enhancement and Service Sector Branding.

www.ingramcontent.com/pod-product-compliance
Lightning Source LLC
Chambersburg PA
CBHW030323020726
47493CB00004B/1133